# WICK

---

## KINGS OF RETRIBUTION MC LOUISIANA

SANDY ALVAREZ

CRYSTAL DANIELS

TWO PENS-

# CRYSTAL *Daniels*

# *Sandy* ALVAREZ

-ONE STORY

# PROLOGUE

## WICK

A rustling sound wakes me from sleep, and I crack my eyes open to see Damien sitting on the edge of his bed, scribbling on a piece of paper. "What the fuck are you doing up? We have to be up in three hours, man."

Damien looks up from his paper. "Can't sleep."

Sitting up, I swing my legs over the side of my bunk, reach down and snag my cigarettes from the pocket of my pants. Placing the cigarette between my lips, I light it and take a drag. "I've noticed you haven't slept much since you got here."

"You know how it is." Damien shrugs.

Damien's unit landed here in Kabul three weeks ago. I was stoked when I found out we would be finishing out our current deployment together. Damien and I graduated from high school together then shipped off to basic training. Three years after joining the service, Damien and I both were deployed to Afghanistan. That was ten years ago. Then Damien and I fulfilled our aspirations two years ago when we officially became Special

Forces. Over the years we served side by side three times. We have eight weeks left with this deployment, and then we get to go home. Damien's lack of sleep this go around is something I have noticed since we've been bunked together. "You want to talk about it?"

The pen in Damien's hand pauses, but he doesn't look up. "Naw. I'm good, man. I'm just restless. Thinking about going home."

I take another drag of my cigarette. "Shit. I hear ya. Eight fuckin' weeks, bro."

Damien and I are silent for a moment before he stops what he's doing and gives me a strange look. "Can I ask you to promise me something, Malik?"

"Of course. You're my best friend, Damien. You name it, and I got your back."

"Promise that if something happens to me, you'll look after Vayda."

My friend's request catches me off guard. I don't want to fathom something happening to him, but because he's my best friend, I agree. "You have my word."

A relieved yet somber look comes over my best friend's face. "I knew I could count on you, Malik."

Damien finishes with what he's writing, folds the paper, and shoves it into an envelope. "One last thing." He pushes the envelope toward me. "In the event I don't make it home, give this to my sister. Give it to her on her wedding day."

A weird feeling settles heavy in my chest at the mention of Vayda getting married. Shaking that thought away, I narrow my eyes at Damien. "You're acting as if something is going to happen to you; like you won't be coming home with me at the end of these eight weeks."

"Look, Malik. I'm sorry I'm suddenly dumping all this heavy shit on you out of the blue. The truth is, I haven't been sleeping well because I got shit on my mind. I'll sleep better knowing my sister is taken care of, and I can't think of a better man for the job than you."

"Fuck, man." I sigh. "Okay. I'm sorry." I take the envelope from his hand. "If something happens, I'll make sure she gets it. But nothing is going to happen. You're going to say whatever is in that letter to Vayda yourself when she marries whatever fucking dickhead she gets with."

"Why do you sound so pissed about my sister's hypothetical husband?" Damien narrows his eyes, but I also see the humor in them.

"Shut up, asshole." I shove the envelope inside my pants pocket and lay back in my bed. "Can we please get some fuckin' sleep now?" What am I supposed to say? Confess to my best friend I have a thing for his baby sister; that suddenly, the thought of her getting married has me wanting to commit murder? Hell, no. I don't see that shit going over well.

Damien's chuckle is the last thing I hear before falling back to sleep.

The next day the sun beatdown on us as we walk through a nearly deserted town. The small village was struck about a month ago, and aside from the few families remaining, the place resembles a ghost town. Casualties were high, and half the town's structures were destroyed. Walking on foot while a Humvee follows us, Damien, and myself, along with a couple of other fellow soldiers patrol the streets keeping vigilant of all potential threats. "I can't fucking wait to get through these next eight weeks. After six months we finally get the chance to go home." Damien says with enthusiasm as he walks beside me.

"Two weeks. That's all we get before they ship our asses off to our next assignment," I remind him.

"Fuck. That's two weeks I get to be with my family, and two weeks I get to spend with my girl back home." Damien grins, bumping my shoulder with his. "You and your folks still plan on celebrating Thanksgiving with us?"

"Yeah. Mom couldn't stop talking about it in the email she sent last week. Her and my dad have my entire two weeks planned out for me when all I want to do is sleep in a decent bed and fill my belly with my mom's home-cookin'." We come to a stop as we walk upon a stalled truck hauling crates filled with chickens in the middle of the narrow road that goes through town. Damien calls out to the two men standing at the front of the truck, who look around the hood at us. "Move!" he yells in their native language. The men look at him before ignoring his command as they continue to whisper amongst themselves before calling back, telling us the truck will not start.

"Shit," I mumble. "Fixing fuckin' broke down hunks of metal hauling smelly ass fowl in the middle of 100-degree weather is not what I signed up for when I wanted to serve my country." Turning to my comrades flanking Damien and myself, I signal I'm going to help so we can continue forward and get our asses back to base. "Come on, let's get this piece of shit moving and out of our way," I tell Damien, and we advance toward the rear of the truck. We don't make it past the back tire when an explosion blinds my vision and propels my body backward, slamming me into a concrete wall.

Disoriented, I look around trying to pinpoint the rest of my team. I shake my head a few times, clearing the cobwebs from my brain.

"Malik!" I faintly hear my name called. "Malik!"

I recognize the detached voice again, before I feel my body being tugged on, and dragged several yards. Damien's face appears in front of mine. He's moving his lips, but through the ringing in my ears I can barely make out what he says. As I come around, and my disorientation dissipates, a searing hot pain like I've never felt before radiates down the entirety of my left side, like someone has melted the flesh from my body. "Shit. Hold on, brother. We're going to get you out of here." Damien does his best to assess my injuries as my teeth grind together and I try to push through the pain.

I look up at my best friend, and notice his headgear missing. "Where the fuck is your helmet, soldier?"

"You're bleeding heavily, Malik." He tells me ignoring my question as he tries to control the bleeding.

"How bad is it?" I ask because I can't look.

"You got this, Malik. You'll be okay."

"If something happens, and I don't make it, tell my family I love them," I tell him, and the heaviness of my words shows on his face.

Damien looks me straight in the eyes. "Shut up. You are not going to die. Not today, brother." He reassures me, just before a bullet rips through his head.

# 1

# WICK

I exit the highway and head in the direction of Twisted Throttle, the bar I co-own with my longtime friend and President of our club, Riggs. The drive from Texas to New Orleans is eight hours. In those eight hours of being alone with my thoughts, I am in no better headspace than I was a week ago when I fled New Orleans to avoid the one woman who has permanently etched herself into my soul. As I pull up in front of the bar, I spot the red KRGT-1 parked between Nova and Fender's bike. I know the smartest thing to do right now would be to turn around and go straight to the clubhouse, but because I love to torture myself, I pull up and park in my usual spot; one of several places reserved for the owners and club members.

Cutting the engine, I stay seated on my bike as I pull a cigarette from my cut and light it. A couple of regular patrons exit the bar and give me a chin lift as they continue down the street. Peering down at my watch, I note it's nearing midnight. Tossing my cigarette to the pavement, I climb off my Midnight Blue custom Fat Bob while ignoring the voice inside my head that urges me to turn my ass around as I stride into the bar. I don't have to seek her out because of how in-tune my body is to hers. My eyes lock on Vayda the second I walk in. As if she can feel my presence, Vayda twists in her seat at the bar and locks eyes with me. Even from across the room, I can see the turmoil swimming in those amber orbs. My fingers twitch at my sides with the need to reach out and touch her. Instead of doing that, I push my needs away and redirect my attention to Riggs, who is handling the bar. I won't lie and say the brief look of hurt that crosses Vayda's face doesn't gut me.

When I sidle up to the bar, my brother senses my mood, and without a word or any nagging questions, he passes me a shot of whiskey and a cold beer. I give him a nod, bring the shot to my lips and ignore the burn as the liquor slides down my throat. Closing my eyes, I get lost in the music filling the room. Sitting on the small stage at the other end of the bar is Fender who is strumming away on his guitar.

There are the days when the vortex of hell threatens to open and take me to the depths of eternal damnation; days when my past and my nightmares swallow me whole and remind me of the demons lurking in the shadows. Today is one of those days. I know it's because of *her*. Seeing Vayda is a constant reminder of how I failed not only Damien, but her.

Vayda showed up a couple of weeks ago when some shit was going down with the club and Prez's woman Luna. She had decided to stay in town and make herself comfortable at the clubhouse. Vayda Wilder has been a friend to the club for several years, but I've known her since she was a kid. Vayda is the little sister of my childhood friend Damien. Vayda, Damien and I grew up together back home in Texas. We both come from military families. When the Wilder's moved into the house next to mine, Mr. Wilder and my parents became instant friends as did me and Damien. My father and Vayda's also worked together. I was an only child whereas Damien had a sister; Vayda. I soon realized wherever Damien was, Vayda wasn't far behind. It wasn't hard to see; she idolized her big brother. In all honesty Damien's little sister tagging along wherever we went didn't bug me. It didn't take long before she became like a sister to me. When Damien and I played on our high school football team together, she was our biggest cheerleader. Not an actual cheerleader because short skirts and pompoms are not Vayda, but she was the loudest one in the bleachers.

I remember one particular game; it was our school's championship game. I scored a touchdown, and when Vayda screamed out my jersey number, I turned toward the stands giving her the biggest grin. I never looked at Vayda with anything more than brotherly affection, but Damien must have seen something on my face at that moment, because he turned to me and said, *"You try anything with my baby sister, and I'll kill you."* Now, mind you, he said those words with a smile on his face, but there was no mistaking the warning in his eyes.

Hearing the unmistakable laughter coming from the end of the bar, I abandon my thoughts of the past and turn my attention to where Vayda is sitting on a stool next to Nova. I clench my fist and grind my teeth at the sight of my brother leaning in close to her then saying something that makes her smile. The beer bottle in my hand threatens to crack under the vise-like grip I have on it —*better this bottle than Nova's head.*

"What the hell are you growling about over here, Wick?" Riggs grunts from behind the bar. "You look like you're about to have a fuckin' stroke."

I give Riggs my best *fuck you* look. He cocks his head and looks down at the end of the bar to where my eyes were trained moments ago. The bastard looks back at me with a shit-eating grin. One I have in mind to knock off his face. "You know he's purposely trying to fuck with you? Cain would never move in on your woman, no matter how big a fuckin' man-whore he is." Cain, who is known to the club as Nova, short for Casanova, for obvious reasons, is Riggs' twin brother. He's also a pain in the ass.

I take a swig of my beer. "I don't know what you're talkin' about, Prez. Vayda is not my woman."

Riggs shakes his head as he takes the empty bottle I shove toward him and tosses it in the trash bin under the bar. "You're so full of shit." Riggs pops the top off a fresh cold beer and sets it down in front of me. I accept it with a scowl. Riggs is calling me out on my lie because he knows me better than anyone and can see straight through my bullshit. I fucking hate it. I've known Riggs since we were in Special Forces together. He is also the only brother who knows about Damien and the day I screwed up and got my best friend killed. "I see it in the way you look at her, brother. I'm also going to take a wild guess and say she's the reason you've been out of town the past week."

I grunt in response. "Just don't take too long pullin' your head out of your ass." With those parting words, Riggs walks off. As much as I hate to admit it, he's not wrong. A week ago, I made the excuse I needed to visit my mom in Texas. The truth was, Vayda being in constant proximity was getting under my skin. I had to leave before I did something stupid. *Like, claim her. Fuck her. Show every motherfucker in this bar she belongs to me.* Chancing another glance at the end of the bar, I meet Vayda's eyes again. Eyes the color of whiskey and sunshine. She's unapologetic in the way she stares at me. The attraction we have for each other is no secret, but if she knew the truth about my role in what happened to her brother, she wouldn't be looking at me the way she is now. My dick hardens against the zipper of my jeans when she brings her beer to her lips, takes a sip then runs her tongue across her bottom lip. Vayda is sexy without having to try. Hell, she makes me hard as a rock by merely breathing the same air as me. Shaking those thoughts away, I tear my gaze away from hers and stand.

"You out of here, brother?" Riggs asks.

"Yeah. I'm beat from the ride home. I'm headed back to the clubhouse." I rap my knuckles on the bar and turn on my heel. It takes all the self-control I can conjure not to look back as I walk out the door of Twisted Throttle.

When I pull up to the clubhouse, which is located next to the river, the club's prospect, Everest who is standing outside and sees me coming, jogs up to the gate and pulls it open, letting me in. Parking, I cut the engine and climb off my bike. "The gate broke again?" I ask Everest.

He nods. "Yeah. The damn thing keeps short-circuiting. Kiwi is going to take a look at it tomorrow."

With a jerk of my chin, I head inside the clubhouse. Everest has been prospecting with The Kings for over a year now and well on his way to earning his patch. Riggs made note after the way Everest handled the situation with Luna; he is going to patch the kid in soon. Everest is currently our only prospect. After Luna's ex Rex Sullivan, the now-dead president of Savage Outlaw killed our other prospect, Track, the club was in no hurry to find a replacement.

When I walk into the clubhouse, Josie greets me with a warm smile from behind the bar. Josie is one of two club girls. She's short and has the kind of curves that will make any man's mouth water. She also sports an abundance of red curly hair. "Hey there, stranger."

"Hey, sweetheart. Where is everybody?" I ask, taking a seat.

Josie tosses the rag she was cleaning with aside and leans her elbows on top of the bar. "They all went out. It's just me, Payton and Everest here tonight." Josie studies me for a beat then asks. "You doing okay, Wick?"

I scrub my hands down my face and note I'm due for a shave. "Been a long couple of weeks, darlin'. That's all."

"Yeah, I can tell. You know I'm here if you want to talk about it." Josie gives me a knowing look. It seems everyone has been able to notice my mood and how Vayda's presence has me rattled. Luckily, Josie changes the subject. "So, how's your momma doing? Did you have a good trip back home?" Josie comes from around the bar and sits on the stool next to me.

"She and Pop are doin' good. Mom finally convinced Pop to take her on that trip to California. I helped them set up their travel arrangements and made sure the neighbors would come by and pick up the mail while they are gone."

"That's great of you, Wick. I hope they have an amazing time." Josie gives me a genuine smile. That's something I admire about both our club girls, Payton and Josie. Both are caring as hell and neither tolerate nor start drama. They are easy-going and take their jobs here at the clubhouse seriously.

Josie slaps her hand on my thigh. "Can I get you a drink or are you turning in for the night?"

I'm about to decline Josie's offer for a drink and head to my room when the door to the clubhouse bursts open. Nova strides through with Vayda sauntering in behind him. Nova continues to make his way toward the bar, whereas Vayda comes to a complete halt. Time stops momentarily as I drink in the sight of her. All 5 feet 8 inches of her. Vayda is wearing a pair of jean shorts that show off her long toned legs and black combat boots. My eyes travel north to where her full breasts strain against the hunter green racerback top she's wearing, then continue upward, where her thick midnight waves kiss the top of her shoulders, before my gaze lands on her eyes. Eyes that at the moment look wounded as they land on my face then quickly dart down to where Josie's hand is resting on my thigh. A look crosses her face before she quickly schools it. Josie must have seen the look too because she removes her hand from me as though she had been burned. I meant it when I said the girls don't cause trouble.

"I'm sorry, Wick," Josie apologizes the same moment Vayda retreats upstairs without a word.

"You have nothin' to be sorry for, sweetheart." I stand and kiss Josie on top of her head. As I make my way across the room and out the door, Nova calls out behind me.

"It's good to see you too, brother."

"Fuck off," I return with the same teasing tone, and it causes Nova to chuckle. I had planned on crashing at the clubhouse tonight, but I don't trust myself with Vayda sleeping under the same roof.

Climbing on my bike, I start her up and rev the engine. When I glance up at the second-story window with the light shining through it, I see Vayda peering down at me. We hold each other's stare for several seconds. She's the first to break the connection this time. Shaking my head, I kick the kickstand up and peel out of the clubhouse parking lot.

The drive to my home is a short one. I live about ten minutes from the clubhouse. I bought my house two years after joining the club. The first time I saw it, I knew I had to have it. I purchased the 1936 Victorian style home for a steal. Riggs had tried to talk me out of buying the dilapidated structure, but I insisted on having it. I didn't tell my friend the real reason I wanted the house. I didn't tell him that when Vayda was thirteen she had a dream of getting married and living in a blue Victorian house with black shutters. She described how she wanted everything down to a T. With help from my brothers we restored the old house in just under a year and a half. The house is three thousand square feet, has four bedrooms, three bathrooms, and a completely updated kitchen with an adjacent sunroom with floor to ceiling windows.

Pulling into the driveway, I steer my bike into the attached garage before climbing off and entering the kitchen through the garage. I flick the light on to my right, illuminating the house then enter the code into the alarm panel. Tossing my keys onto the counter, I round the kitchen island and head toward the refrigerator. Pulling it open, I sigh when I see nothing but empty shelves and a few bottles of beer. Swiping one from the shelf, I pop the top and take a swig as I stride into the archway of the living room. I stop and stare at the vast empty space. My entire house sits empty—all except my bedroom, and a small table in the kitchen.

Several of my brothers have ribbed on me from time to time asking why I have this big ass house but haven't bothered to fill it. My excuse is always the same; I don't have the time. The truth is, I don't feel right finishing it. This place is Vayda's dream. A part of me feels it's not my place. The sick twisted thing about the whole situation is that she has no idea this place exists.

She'd probably think I was crazy if she knew. I mean, Vayda probably doesn't even remember the conversation she had with me at thirteen.

Shaking memories of the past away, I walk through the living room and make my way up the stairs to the end of the hall to my bedroom. I shrug my cut off and drape it over the chair next to the bed.

Walking into the en-suite bathroom to take a shower, I strip out of my t-shirt and jeans and toss them to the floor. Standing in front of the mirror, I look at the scars that run across the left side of my abdomen and trail along my ribs around to my back. My scars are jagged and angry looking. They also serve as a reminder of the worst day of my life. The day the devil himself paid me a visit and forever altered my future.

Once finished with my shower, I put on a pair of gray sweats and make my way over to the desk I have set up in front of the window. Knowing sleep won't come easy tonight, I decide to fire up the computer and do the books for the club and the bar. When I left active duty at age thirty, I dove headfirst into furthering my education. By the time I graduated high school, I had several colleges offering me scholarships, including Columbia. School was not my calling, though. Serving my country is what I wanted to do with my life. As soon as my dream ended, I poured all my ambition into something I excelled at when in school. I had always been good with numbers. Numbers make sense to me. So, without hesitation, I went back to school and got my bachelor's degree in Mathematics from the University of California-Berkeley. It took me four years to finish my degree. Once I had finished with school, I didn't know what direction I was headed next.

It was then Riggs came back into my life. Riggs and I served together in my last two years of Special Forces. We had stayed connected here and there once I left the service, but when he called me up one day and invited me down to New Orleans, I jumped at the chance to catch up with my friend. Once I got here, Riggs filled me in on what he had been doing with his life. How he had been living in Montana and joined the MC. Soon after he joined The Kings his grandfather fell ill, and he had to leave his club behind for long periods of time.

The Kings of Retribution founding President, Jake Delane put an offer on the table; one Riggs couldn't turn down. Open a second chapter here in Louisiana. Riggs' first call was to me. He said there was no other man he wanted by his side. He offered me the position as his Vice President. I accepted in a heartbeat. I knew then, and there The Kings of Retribution was my destiny. I will forever be grateful to Riggs and my brothers. My club gives me purpose. I would lay down my life for my brothers and know they would do the same for me.

# 2

# TEQUILA

After sleeping like shit most of the night, I decide to grab a quick shower so I can head down to the gun range.

Maybe a few rounds of target practice will help defuse my anger. Who am I trying to fool? I'm fighting mad because jealousy has a hold on me after seeing Malik with one of the club girls.

Taking the guys up on an earlier offer, I load up my gear, strap it to the back of my bike, and take off toward town. Once I get to the tactical store the club owns, I park my bike alongside the others. Slinging my bag over my shoulder, I make my way inside, immediately spotting Everest behind the counter. "Hey, Tequila."

Greeting him with a smile, I ask. "The guys in the back?"

"Yeah. Head on back." He goes about his business, and I cross the room, opening the door leading to the indoor gun range located on the backside of the store. It's actually the first time I've taken the time to use the gun range since Riggs and his men opened the place. Rounding the corner, I come upon a smaller room separated by a large window that overlooks the range. Spotting Nova, Fender, and Kiwi, I place my gear on the bare table sitting in the room and unpack my weapon. With it strapped to my side, and a couple of boxes of ammunition in my hand, I enter the shooting range.

Nova spots me. Sitting his gun down, he removes his ear protection, letting the earphones hang around his neck. "Hey, beautiful. Come to show off some of your infamous shooting skills we've all heard so much about?" He gives me his signature panty-dropping grin.

"You scared I'm going to come in here and show you, boys, how it's done?" I taunt him, having a little fun.

"Those are fighting words."

Looking unimpressed, I shrug my shoulders and pretend to admire my nails. "I win; you owe me a drink and get to wash and polish my bike."

"Only if you're willing to do the same when you lose." He wagers.

"Sure."

"Show me what you got," Nova grins, playing right along with me.

Stepping into one of the partitioned spaces, I place my weapon and ammo on the shelf in front of me and begin to load my firearm. It doesn't take long for Kiwi and Fender to join us.

"Aww hell." I look over my left shoulder, and Fender is rubbing his palms together. "We're about to watch Nova get his ass kicked."

"Hold up," Kiwi chimes in. "We need to document this shit." Glancing past Fender, I notice Kiwi holding his phone in the air and I laugh.

With a new target hanging, I keep the safety engaged on my firearm and step to the side. With a gesture for Nova to take my place I tell him, "Ladies first."

Being a good sport, Nova throws his head back in laughter. "Let the master show you how to do it." He strides up, taking my place, and pulls his weapon from its holster. Aiming, he shoots three rounds. Laying his gun down, he presses the button to his right, and the target floats down the alley in our direction. Nova stops it a couple of feet in front of us and folds his arms across his chest.

I nod. "Not bad." I take in his shots. Two in the head and one in the upper chest area. "Not bad at all," I repeat, impressed by his ability. "Send it back."

Pressing the button, the silhouette becomes smaller as it moves backward. He stops it about midway, just a tad closer than what he had it. "Keep going." I raise my brow, and he smirks, while Fender and Kiwi snicker behind us. Only when the target hits the end of the track and can't go any further do I tell him. "That's good."

Nova steps to the side, and I take my stance. Holding my weapon in front of me, I line up my target and squeeze the trigger. After firing several rounds, I holster my gun and push the retrieval button. The closer it gets, I grin. I put a couple bullets through each mark Nova made, widening the holes he already put through the paper before emptying the rest of my clip into the center of the silhouette.

"Holy shit, man. You see how clean those shots are?" Fender pokes his finger through the bullet hole in the center. "You put each bullet through the previous mark with precision."

Nova pulls the target from the clip. "Fuck." He turns to Kiwi. "Did you get all that?"

"Damn right, I did." Kiwi beams.

"Good." Nova turns back toward me. "That was impressive fuckin' shootin'. As impressive as your drinking skills. Or so I've heard."

"Thanks." The men follow me to the other room, where I grab a bottle of cold water from my bag. "You plan on challenging me on those skills too?" I twist the cap of the bottle.

"Drinking?" Nova looks at me. "Hell no. I've heard all about your drinkin' skills. Save your game for some other fool who doesn't know any better."

After taking a drink of my water, I reply, "Riggs must have told you."

"Wait a minute. Does this story have anything to do with the origin of your nickname, Tequila?" Kiwi chimes in, and I nod. "I need to hear this one. You care to share?"

I shrug my shoulders. "Not much to tell. One weekend, while on a short leave between missions, I went out with a few of the guys. A simple drinking game turned into a competition between us and another unit. We got to choose one man from their group and vice versa. Of course, they decided who they thought would be the weakest link." I pause, and grab another firearm from my bag, placing the one I just shot in its case. "Anyway, they chose Tequila as their poison of choice. I went up against a soldier the size of a refrigerator. First one to puke loses." I grin, thinking back to that night. "Their man lost." Little do they know I paid the price all night when I went back to my base housing.

Heading back into the gun range, the three of us spend another hour shooting and cutting up with each other. It proved to be the medicine I needed to melt away my stress, and half-ass forget about Malik for a while.

Walking outside with the guys, I strap my bag down and swing my leg over my bike. Nova slides his shades on after doing the same. "How about we carry our asses over to Twisted Throttle," Nova says while looking at me. "I owe you a drink, and a bike wash."

Two weeks. That's how long its been since my last mission, so I shouldn't complain that I'm on my way to the clubhouse to pack my shit and head out after getting a call from Scott. I've been serving my country since I graduated high school. Still considered active duty, most of my missions have become covert. During one of those missions is when I met Riggs, and Malik happened to be serving alongside him. Since then I've piloted several more missions with them.

I've spent my time off the past couple of weeks here in New Orleans, alongside my second family, The Kings of Retribution MC. I've even seen some action; meaning I beat a bitch my first night in town, but hey, what can I say? *Laissez Les Bon temp rouler.*

Then there's Malik, or Wick as his brother's call him. There's a ray of sunshine for you. Sucking the fun right out of the room whenever I wanted to have a good time. He and Riggs own a bar on Bourbon Street called Twisted Throttle. There is always live music, and my drinks have been free. That is until Malik decides I've had enough and cuts me off. *Killjoy.* That, and any man who so much as looked my way he managed to scare off with his murderous stare. *Who the hell does he think he is anyway?* He doesn't want me. He made that abundantly clear long ago.

Twisting the throttle, I pick up speed, the hot, humid wind licks at my bare skin as I travel down the road. The entire situation between Malik and I is, well, complicated. The memory and taste of his kiss cause my thighs to flex against the vibration of the bike between my legs. The kiss which happened during a mission more than a year ago. The very one Malik also said was a mistake. Pushing my bike a little harder, I do my best to avoid the rush of emotions trying to suck the life out of me.

Slowing to a stop, I punch in the security code and wait for the massive metal gate to roll open, then pull my bike alongside Malik's. "Great," I roll my eyes as I kill the engine. Relief washes over me the moment I walk through the front door and find the common area empty. Doing my best to avoid running into Malik, I jog up the stairs, heading straight for my room. Knowing *his* is two doors down the hall, I make quick work of shoving what few things I brought with me inside my duffle bag.

Stopping briefly, I glance at myself, in the full-length mirror leaning against the wall beside the bedroom door; my skin still glistening with sweat from the heat of the Louisiana summer. Unblinking, I catch small glimpses of my brother staring back at me. Not a day passes without thinking of Damien. It's been eleven years since we lost him, but some days, it feels like it was only yesterday when I watched a black sedan pull into our driveway.

Closing my eyes, I fight back the tears and swallow my emotions.

"Running away?" Malik's gravelly voice pierces the silence, dragging me from my memories.

Opening my eyes, I find him leaning against the doorframe, his large frame taking up the entire width of the opening. For a moment, I become fixed on his earthy brown eyes, and the way the sunlight coming through the bedroom window catches warm hues of copper surrounding his pupils. "I've never run from anything." Without hiding behind an indifferent stare and falsities, my eyes travel the length of his body. Wearing black jeans, black combat boots, and nothing beneath his cut, I drink him in like a cold glass of sweet tea until my eyes connect with his once more. The smell of perfume hits my nose the moment I take a step toward him, reminding me of yesterday, and how relaxed and engaging he was with Josie. I shouldn't let it bother me, but it does. Masking my jealousy, I fling my bag over my shoulder. "Scott called, I have an intel briefing at 2200." Malik takes a step back, allowing me to step into the hall. I feel his presence behind me as I descend the stairs.

"You know where he's sending you?" Malik questions as he follows.

"Nope." Keeping pace, I cross the room. "You know how Scott works. He gives us nothing until we get to his location."

"You plan on seeing your dad before you head out?"

With my hand wrapped around the handle of the door, I pull it open and soften when he mentions my daddy. "Yeah."

"Give him my best. Let him know I plan on visiting soon." Malik's hand grips the door just above my head.

Looking over my shoulder, I smile. I can be mad at Malik for a lot of things, but he cares for my dad like he is his own. And that alone means everything to me. "I will." Turning, I head towards my bike, leaving Malik standing in the doorway. I feel him watching me while I secure my bag, pull my hair back, slip my helmet over my head, then swing my leg over my bike.

"Vayda," Malik calls out, and I make eye contact with him. "Stay safe."

"Always."

After hours on the road, I make it to Scott's place, not his home, but his base of operations. I also notice the other three vehicles parked nearby and immediately know who I'm working with on this mission. After parking my bike alongside his black Jeep, I head for the side entrance found on the side of the building and push the button on one of those doorbells equipped with a camera.

A deep voice comes through the speaker. "Whatever you're selling, I'm buying, sugar." I break out in a smile, then hear the door locks disengage, and I pull it open. Inside I find Travis aka Cowboy leaning back in his chair, with his booted feet kicked up on the tabletop in front of the security monitors. He gives me a good look over before standing. "It's been a minute. How are you doing, sugar?" He greets me with a warm smile before embracing me.

"I'm good."

"Aww, hell." Another voice echoes off the concrete wall. Turning, I see Burks, whom we call Preacher due to the fact he carries The Bible wherever he goes. Entering the room behind him is Thorstad, but his friends call him Thor. "Tequila." Preacher strides across the room, and I cast a smile his way.

"Preacher, I thought you were hanging up your boots," I mention knowing his sister's illness has taken its toll on him. And knowing cancer can affect the entire family, I would understand if he walked away from all of this for good.

"Now that Ariel is responding to treatment, she insisted I get back out there." His eyes light up as he thinks about her, and my heart hurts a little because I miss having that connection with Damien.

"Your sister is a strong young woman. If anyone can kick cancer's ass, it will be her," I say wholeheartedly. Glancing past Preacher's shoulder, I give a wave to Thor. "Hey, big guy." "Good to see you, Tequila." He gives a quick nod.

"Well, now that the four of you have had your little family reunion, let's get the show on the road." Scott walks into the room with a six pack of beer in one hand and a stack of files in the other.

Gathering around the small card table in the center of the room, Scott passes the beers around as we pull out the chairs and take a seat. He then proceeds to hand each of us a file. "Satellite images appear to have uncovered a small camp belonging to the Cartel in Mexico on the other side of the Rio Grande. One of our sources tells us they have several young women who are currently being held in this location."

"These fucking piles of human waste make me sick." Cowboy scowls as he sifts through the images in his file. Young girls that look to be no older than eighteen, with guns pointed at them as they are led into an old storage building. "I'd like to hogtie every one of them, castrate them, shove their dicks down their throats and watch them choke," he fumes, closing the folder.

"However, the women are not the reason for this mission. At least not top priority to our clients." Scott elaborates and anger rises between the four of us.

"What the hell, Scott?" I fume.

His hand goes up in defense. "Hear me out. You and I both know getting the women out will be a top priority, but these men are part of a much larger organization. The head man himself, Arturo Cortez, owns the property in question." Scott informs us.

"Arturo *The Butcher* Cortez?" I look up from the aerial images laid out in front of me. My blood runs cold. This guy is ruthless. He's known as The Butcher, well, because he butchers those who cross him. Word is, he gets off on it too. The sick fuck.

"Exactly," Scott clarifies. "He has these women right in his own backyard. We not only get those women out of there, but we take him down in the process. We take out one of the top three drug lords and human traffickers in the world." All of us glance at one another. This is a big fucking deal. This mission just turned into much more than an in and out rescue. We are being asked to help take down one of the largest Cartels in history.

After spending the next couple of hours going over every detail of our mission, I get the okay to cut out for a couple of hours before I'm needed to return. Hopping on my bike, I drive thirty five minutes until I'm pulling into a familiar driveway. The front door opens before I cut the engine, and my dad steps out onto the front porch. My entire being relaxes the moment I walk up the steps and into his waiting arms. "Hey, Daddy."

"Hey, Pumpkin. I was wondering when you'd come to see me." He gives me a final squeeze before pulling back. "Let me have a look at you."

"I don't look any different than I did four weeks ago." I laugh, then grow somber. "I can't stay long." And my dad eyes me for a minute, waiting for me to divulge more information. "I leave first thing in the morning." He knows what I do, and being ex-military he knows I can't discuss it further.

"I have leftovers in the refrigerator. At least stay for dinner." He walks inside, and I follow. "So, how's Scott?" he asks as I close the door and follow him to the kitchen.

"He's good."

Dad nods while he reaches inside the refrigerator; pulling out leftover ribs and a bowl of mac and cheese. "How was New Orleans? And Malik?"

And there it is. I was wondering how long it would take for

him to ask. "Good times," I say with a little too much cynicism in my tone. "Malik says hello, and he plans to visit soon."

My dad sighs. "This has been going on for too long, Pumpkin. Now, I don't know what is going on between you and Malik, but I wish you two would work it out."

"There is nothing between us, Daddy."

"Bullshit." He sits our plates on the table after warming them in the microwave and waits for me to take my seat. "There's something off between the two of you. I hear it in your voice when you speak of the other person."

I pick up my fork. "Daddy, I didn't come here to get a lecture where Malik is concerned," I say with a little too much sass.

"Vayda." My dad cuts me a look I know all too well, letting me know I need to rein in the attitude.

"Sorry, Daddy."

He rests his hand on my arm. "Pumpkin. You've known each other for a long time. Whatever it is, work it out. Malik is a good man. He may never admit it, but your friendship is important to him."

I stew on his words as we eat our meals. I wish it were that simple. My dad is right. Malik is a good man; always has been. But Malik is fighting what we both want. He's running from his feelings—from me. And as much as I'd like to share that with my dad, I can't.

# 3

# WICK

Hey, Wick!" Kiwi calls out from over by the pool table. "Get your arse over here in this game, man. I want to play against some real competition."

"Fuck you, asshole." Nova flips Kiwi the bird, clearly offended by his remark.

"Just statin' a fact, brother," Kiwi continues to goad. "Don't get all sensitive on me, mate."

Chuckling, I stand from my seat at the bar and stride across the room. "The only game you have, Nova, is with women."

Nova grins at my statement. "Pussy game is the only game that matters. Speaking of..." Nova tosses his pool cue at me, and I catch it. "I need to go see a doctor about the ache in my balls."

I shake my head as I watch Nova's retreating form walk out the door of the clubhouse. My brother has a whole goddamn harem, one of which is Dr. Teagan.

"You can break," Kiwi says when I turn my attention back to the game. Once Kiwi has the balls in place, I lean over the table to take my shot. Just as I have my cue lined up, my cell rings. Straightening, I set the stick down and retrieve my phone from the inside of my cut. Looking at the screen, I see it's Riggs calling. "Prez?" With it being nearly midnight, I know he's not calling to chat.

"I need you down at the bar, now," he barks into the phone, his tone putting me on high alert.

"What's going on, brother?" Out of the corner of my eye, I see Kiwi set his pool stick down and step closer.

"I'll explain when you get here," he says the same moment I hear sirens in the distance before the line goes dead.

"Something is up down at the bar," I say over my shoulder as Kiwi follows me outside where we mount our bikes. Together we fire up our bikes and peel out of the compound in the direction of Twisted Throttle.

With Kiwi riding alongside me on the left, we turn the corner of St Ann Street. Kiwi and I give each other the same puzzling look as we come upon the scene in front of the bar. Several police cruisers along with a fire truck and ambulance line the street. I park a few yards away, hop off my bike and haul ass in the direction of the officer who is currently talking to Riggs and standing next to him, is his woman, Luna. I'm about ten feet from Riggs when an officer, I don't recognize, steps in front of me and places his palm on my shoulder, halting my movements. "This is a potential crime scene. You can't be here."

Grabbing the motherfucker by his wrist, I twist his arm, bringing it behind his back, sending him to his knees. Already knowing what the young officer's next move will be, I place my booted foot over the hand he has braced on the ground. "This potential crime scene is about to become a fuckin' murder scene if you put your goddamn hands on me again," I spew.

The officer's face turns red from anger and humiliation. "You're going to be placed under arrest for assaulting a police officer."

Applying a bit more pressure to his wrist for good measure, I smirk down at the asshole. "I don't think I will."

The cop looks around at his colleagues. Not one of them is making a move to help him or arrest me. When my gaze lands on the Chief himself, he has an exasperated look on his face as he strolls in our direction. New Orleans' Chief of Police stops in front of me and rests his hands on his utility belt. "Think you can let my rookie up there, Wick?" he says in a bored tone.

"No problem, Chief." I release my hold on the cop. The fucker goes to say something, but Chief Richards stops him.

"Look, son. I know you're new around here, but this man right here is the Vice President of The Kings of Retribution. It will do you good to remember the names and the faces of each man in their club. I may not be there to save your ass the next time you make such a careless mistake."

"You're telling me the force is tangled up with these criminals?" the guy stupidly continues.

Scoffing at his use of the word criminals, I go to lunge for the asshole. Chief Richards cuts me off. "These so-called criminals as you like to put it are the very reason we can keep the streets of New Orleans clean. Two of these so-called criminals are U.S. veterans; men who served this country with integrity and respect. These criminals also hold a charity run every year to raise money for our local school to ensure each child's lunch is paid for the year, and no child is without school supplies." By this point, the Chief is fuming, but he continues. "These so-called criminals also offer up their gun range to the force; free of charge since ours burned down two years ago." By the time Chief Richards is finished with his ass chewing it's clear the rookie is embarrassed, and it's taking all his strength to bite his tongue. "Now get your ass out of here and do your job."

Not giving the situation a second thought, I regard the Chief with a nod and make my way toward Riggs. This is not the first time someone will assume shit about the club, and it won't be the last. We're not choir boys but we also don't run shit that could get us killed anymore either. The Kings have been straight for a couple years now. The Kings used to have our hands in a lot of illegal shit, but not as much in the past three or four years. The Kings are more about the brotherhood and helping our community. There are times when we are not on the same side as the law, but our local boys in blue tend to mind their own business in those situations.

"Did ya have to be so rough on the newbie, brother?" Riggs jests when I step in front of him.

"He needed to learn his place." I shrug. "Now tell me what the hell happened here, Prez."

Riggs runs his hand through his beard and lets out a heavy sigh before turning to his woman, who is still standing by his side. Riggs puts his hands out in front of him and signs something to Luna, who is deaf. He speaks out loud as he does. "I want you to go upstairs with Fender. I have something I need to take care of."

Without question, Luna nods and follows Fender back inside the bar. With Luna gone, I push my previous question.

"Talk to me, Riggs."

"We had a guy overdose in the men's bathroom tonight. Fender found him."

"Is he dead?"

Riggs shakes his head. "He wasn't breathin' when Fender found him. I administered CPR until the ambulance showed up. The paramedics called it about ten minutes ago. The kid was only twenty-five."

"Fuckin hell," Kiwi mutters.

My blood starts to boil as one-word rips from my mouth. "Kostas."

Kostas has been a thorn in our side for over a year now. He's been peddling his drugs on the streets of New Orleans while ignoring multiple warnings from the club. He's also failed to heed

Riggs' threat the last time we caught his minions in Twisted Throttle a couple of months ago.

"Wick." Riggs calls my name, snapping me out of my thoughts. "Call Everest. Tell him I need him down here to keep an eye on Luna. I also want you to tell Nova to get his ass out of whatever pussy he's in and get to the bar. We're going to pay a visit to Kostas." Riggs steps away to talk with Chief Richards while I pull my cell from my pocket and fire off a text to both Nova and Everest. They both reply immediately saying they are on their way.

Thirty minutes later Everest and Nova arrive, and the street in front of the bar is now void of emergency vehicles. I sit on my bike smoking a cigarette as I wait for Riggs to come down from the apartment he shares with Luna that's located on the second floor of Twisted Throttle. Myself along with my other brothers, Kiwi, Fender, and Nova, stay silent. As we wait, we meet each other's eyes and share a look. We are through playing nice with Kostas.

When Riggs rounds the corner of the bar, I flick my cigarette to the ground and fire up my bike. I feel my adrenaline kicking in as my Prez and brothers follow suit. I wait for Riggs to back out of his space and pull out onto the road before I ride up beside him while Kiwi, Fender and Nova fall into formation behind us. Riggs raises his hand in the air, giving his men the signal to expect trouble. He then peers over at me with a look I know all too well; one that says shit is about to go down. I give him a chin lift, letting him know I am more than fucking ready.

The first thing the club did when Kostas moved his dealing into New Orleans was find out where all three of his drop houses were located. Word is he bounces around between the three houses daily. And if I know my Prez like I think I do; we will be hitting all three houses tonight until we find him. Kostas thinks The Kings were playing when we told him to take his drugs somewhere else, but tonight he's about to learn a valuable lesson, and that is you don't fuck with the club or our town.

It only takes about ten minutes for us to arrive at the first house. I want to laugh when the two guys sitting on the porch dash inside the front door upon our arrival. Not wasting any time, myself along with Riggs and my other brothers roll our bikes right up onto the lawn, coming to a stop at the front door. The moment we climb off our bikes and draw our weapons, a large Latino man and a skinny white dude step out of the house. The larger man has his beefy arms crossed over his chest while trying to look intimidating. I recognize the skinny asshole more the closer I get to him. He is the same asshole we kicked out of Twisted Throttle a couple of months back. The asshole looks nervous as fuck too. He's also fidgeting too much for my liking. Riggs nor I say a single word as we climb the steps of the porch. We are not here to make niceties; we are here to ask questions. And our way of questioning usually involves blood.

"What the hell do you want?" The big fucker tries to block mine and Riggs' entry into the house. I ignore his question by slamming my fist into his gut, then delivering an uppercut to his jaw. The asshole goes down hard and when his body hits the railing of the porch, the wood splinters, sending him falling backward to the ground below, knocking him out cold. Next, I turn my attention to Riggs who has the tweaker by the scruff of his neck, forcing him through the front door. When we step inside, I see Fender, Kiwi, and Nova have already made it through the backdoor and have their pieces drawn on the two other fuckers sitting on a sofa in the living room; both looking like they are seconds away from pissing their pants.

"Where the fuck is Kostas?" Riggs demands shoving the guy he's holding toward the sofa where he falls over his buddies.

"He's not here," one of the guys who doesn't look a day over twenty offers. It's a fucking shame these young kids throw their life away on bullshit like this.

"No shit, he's not here," I bark. "I believe my Prez was asking you dipshits where he is."

This time it's the tweaker who pipes up. "Kostas doesn't tell us shit. He only comes by once a day to collect his money. And if it's not him, he sends one of his bodyguards."

"Has he collected from this house tonight?" I ask.

Tweaker goes to open his mouth to answer but is cut off by one of the other guys. This one looks to be older than the other two, at least in his mid-thirties and has stringy blond hair. "Shut the fuck up, Pete. You know how Kostas feels about snitches. He'll kill us."

Raising my gun, I fire a single shot into the blond motherfucker's leg. He squeals in pain while his two friends look on in shock. My brothers, however, don't even flinch. "Looks like you assholes are at an impasse, because *I'll* kill you if you don't talk." I keep my eyes trained on the guy I shot. He's obviously in pain and starting to sweat bullets. He takes a moment to contemplate what to do before he makes the wise choice of opening his mouth. "Kostas is due to stop by at 2:00," he grits through clenched teeth.

Peering down at my watch, I note the time. "We have twenty minutes," I say to Riggs. With my gun still trained on the three men, Riggs holsters his weapon and nods toward Kiwi, Fender, and Nova. "Let's move our bikes around back. Wick, you stay put and watch these fuckers."

"You got it, Prez."

A few minutes later, Riggs and the other brothers make their way back inside; with them the big dude I knocked out on the porch. "Sleeping beauty decided to wake up," Kiwi jests.

"Take a seat with your friends, princess." I point my gun and motion toward the sofa. The guy gives me a murderous glare as he stumbles his way across the room. I note the swelling coupled with the bruising on his face. I smirk.

The twenty-minutes we had to wait for Kostas turned into only ten. My guess is he was tipped off to our arrival. Peeking out the blinds, I watch as a black SUV pulls up and parks on the road in front of the house. One guy exits the driver side as a second climbs out of the front passenger seat then opens the back door for a guy in a suit. I assume this is Kostas himself. Turning away from the window, I regard Riggs who is looking every bit as chill sitting at the kitchen table smoking a cigarette while Kiwi stands guard at the back door. Fender and Nova took their leave five minutes ago to make sure Kostas didn't have any of his men catch us off guard by coming up behind the house. When I turn back to look out the window, I note Kostas and his two men walking up the steps of the porch. The three of them stop in their tracks when they see the busted banister. Kostas nods to the guy on his right and motions for him to walk through the front door first. *Pussy.*

Just as the front door opens, I raise my gun, pointing at the head of the guy who walks in first. He goes to reach for his weapon when I spit out, "That would be a terrible fuckin' move." The guy halts his movements. "Get your ass inside," I order.

Slowly the guy makes his way fully into the house with Kostas and his second guard following behind. Kostas himself makes an ill-fated mistake by opening his mouth. "It would be wise of you and your friends to walk away now." No sooner does the threat leave his mouth when the butt of my pistol comes down on the side of his face, the blow causing his brow to split open and blood to gush from the wound. Riggs is the next to speak.

"You seem to think you have a say in what goes on in my town. And you have a big set of balls thinkin' you can talk shit and spew orders, motherfucker." By this point Prez has stood from his seat and stepped directly in front of Kostas. "You failed to heed my warning the first time you had your peddlers pushing drugs in my bar. Then tonight a man dies from an overdose in Twisted Throttle's bathroom. Now, I'm tellin' you face to face that your operation here in New Orleans is shut down, effective immediately."

Kostas chuckles. "You and your club are pussies. You're a bunch of do-gooder bikers who pretend you have control over this city. New Orleans belongs to me now." Kostas stops talking long enough to make his second biggest mistake of the night. One I know is about to cost him his life. He spits on the top of Riggs' boot. I notice the tick in my brother's jaw and the twitch of his trigger finger; two signs that tell me how this night is going to end. I keep my gun aimed at the guy standing to Kostas's right. Kiwi swiftly makes his way to my side, and aims his piece at the man as well. In a blink of an eye, Riggs makes his move by pulling his gun from the inside of his cut, places the barrel to the front of Kostas's forehead and pulls the trigger. Blood and brain matter paint the front door behind him. When the fucker in front of me gets a look on his face that says he's thinking about doing something stupid to avenge his former boss, I step forward separating the distance between us and press my gun against his temple. "You prepared to meet your maker today, motherfucker?" The guy's Adam's apple bobs when he swallows and shakes his head no.

Looking around the room at the rest of Kostas's goons, I ask, "Do we have a problem here?"

Everyone shakes their heads. Satisfied with their answers, I turn to Riggs and nod. "Prez."

Riggs eyes the dead man on the floor then the shitheads sitting on the sofa. "The five of you have until sunup to spread the word about your boss then get the fuck out of New Orleans."

A few hours later, I'm sitting in Riggs' office at the clubhouse. It's just past 5:00 am when Kiwi, Fender, and Nova come strolling in. "Is it done?" Riggs asks.

"All taken care of, Prez," Fender says, taking a seat in the chair next to me while Nova and Kiwi plop down on the sofa.

I ask the next question. "They leave town?"

"Sure did," Kiwi chuckles. "They lit out of here like their arses were on fire. Fuckin' pussies."

"And the other?" I continue.

Kiwi's face turns serious before he nods. "Taken care of."

Prez had instructed Kiwi and Nova to hit up the other two drop houses Kostas was using to peddle his drugs and confiscate any money found. We also found out where Kostas was living and found a fuck ton of cash in a safe there. The payment was then dropped off anonymously at the parents' house of the young man who died from the overdose. It turns out the kid was a law student who had become addicted to speed then later graduated to the harder stuff. It's a goddamn shame how easily that shit can be obtained. Hopefully now with Kostas off the streets of New Orleans we can avoid another life gone too soon.

Once my brothers have taken their leave, I stand from my seat. "Need anything else from me, Prez? I'm going to head home and try to get a couple of hours of sleep. You still need me to open the bar tonight?"

"Yeah, brother, if ya don't mind. I have plans with Luna."

"You got it." I give him a chin lift. As I'm walking out of his office, Riggs stops me.

"Malik?"

"Yeah?"

"Thanks for having my six back there."

"Always, brother."

# 4

# TEQUILA

*I am not a morning person.*

The piercing sound of my alarm has me knocking the clock from the box crate sitting beside the cot I had the luxury of sleeping on last night. Lying on my stomach, I mumble incoherently into the pillow. The smell of strong, freshly brewed coffee coaxes my eyelids open.

"Rise and shine, sugar," Cowboy says with a Texas draw strong enough to drop panties yet does nothing to quench my thirst. Only one man has that much control over me.

Rolling onto my side, I proceed to sit on the edge of my cot and take the steaming mug from Cowboy's outstretched arm. "You're the best." I take a sip and look through my lashes to find him wearing a devilish grin that only Cowboy could get away with.

"That's what I've been told." He says with confidence. All I can do is smile and shake my head. "Let's shit and git', Wilder. The rest of us are geared up." He looks down at his watch. "Roll out in ten, soldier."

Less than ten minutes later, I have my gear packed, and I'm ready to go. It's a thirty-minute drive to a secure location, on private property, where we roll up to a modest-sized hanger. As we exit the SUV, the hanger doors begin to open, and a small jeep tows the evac helicopter I'll be flying. "How the fuck did you get your hands on one of these?" I question in astonishment as I take her in. I make a complete walk around the aircraft before coming to stand next to my comrades who are loading the necessary supplies.

"The government wants this guy." Scott pats the side panel where he is standing. "It's on loan until we complete the mission. Along with the cash payout you each will receive. It's all part of the package. Once the mission is completed, it's ours."

Not ignoring the fact that specific organizations funding this project are more focused on the criminal himself than the victims, I throw my arms across my chest. "The money means jack shit. Those women and children he's selling are the main reason I'm not backing out of this entirely. As long as I can get them out..."

Scott interrupts me mid-rant. "Nevertheless, you chose to take on this mission." His features soften a bit. Scott has been doing mercenary work for a long time. The missions he takes on don't always fall into the moral category, but he still has his reasons for doing them. With this one, though bigger heads have made it clear what their priorities are, we all know it is the future victims who really matter. I toss my only bag on top of the other gear being strapped down.

Pulling the cockpit door open, I climb in and get myself familiar with the feel and layout when Scott appears at my side. "Be careful. I know it's been a while since you've been in the field." Turning my body, I face him. "Keep our boys in line for me and bring those women home." He solidifies the reason I like being a part of his team.

"Yes, sir," I smile at him, before fastening the seatbelts across my chest, and he walks away.

"Listen up." Cowboy is the last to climb in. "I know this is last minute, but Scott just received this new intel moments ago himself. Landing coordinates have changed." He hands me a piece of paper. "There's been some new activity, so we'll be heading upriver by a few miles. Which means we have a long trek to reach our destination."

Once our new coordinates are logged, I slip my headgear on and turn on the headset. With preflight rituals out of the way, I start the engine, bringing the helicopter to life. I can't explain the feelings I get in the pit of my stomach with every takeoff I make. Unless you've piloted an aircraft yourself, you couldn't understand the rush behind it. Lifting into the sky, I tune into the hum of the propellers whirling, and make a smooth turn to the south as I navigate us toward Mexico.

Silence falls upon the cabin—all of us in our own headspaces with our own thoughts. Mine happen to be all over the place this morning. I'm thinking about the women we are after and hope like hell they are still alive by the time we extract them. Then, I think about the dirtbags who took them in the first place, stealing their lives away from them. Each cell—each human trafficking ring has its own way of doing things. Anyone is a potential victim and a payday to them. They don't care if you're rich, poor, women, or children. All they see is dollar signs. The highest bidder wins the prize. Sometimes, when they've kidnapped someone of wealthy origins, they ask for ransom. Unfortunately, those scenarios never end well. The family is so eager to meet the demands, and rightfully so that they act quickly without inside help. Like so many countless families, they are guaranteed never to see their loved ones again. Traffickers take the money, then sell the person anyway. Or worse—they kill them.

I've seen all the ugly sides to human life being bartered and sold like cattle. And I mean that in all literal sense. Some of the traffickers brand the bodies of their victims. We've rescued many lives in the years I've been doing these missions, and it never gets any easier. But it shouldn't. I don't ever want to become jaded in what I do—what we do. I never want it to become just another job. Their lives mean more to me than that.

Under the cloak of darkness, I fly just above the horizon where the veil of the dawn sky kisses the surface of the earth. "ETA twenty minutes, boys." I break the silence amongst us. The atmosphere changes with preparations. Adrenaline kicks into high gear the closer we get. Following the river, we close in on our drop point. "You see anything?" I ask Preacher, who is using an expensive ass piece of night vision equipment with the ability and range to see all ground movement below us.

"Negative. You're clear to land." He confirms, and I make my descent.

"Nervous?" Cowboy's hand squeezes my shoulder.

I laugh. "Maybe just a little. It's been a minute since I've been a part of the ground team. I'm usually on standby for drop off and pick up. I sit with my aircraft. This time, we are taking a huge risk leaving her half-ass hidden." With precision, I set us down, just behind an old abandoned barn about thirty yards from the edge of the river nearby.

"We need you on this one, Tequila. Regardless of who we are supposed to take out on this mission, I plan to find those women he is holding. I'm going to need your help convincing them it's okay to trust us so we can get them out of here. With everything that can go wrong on this one, we can't afford to waste precious time," Cowboy explains.

Turning, I take off my gear. "Ready when you are," I tell him, then climb out of the cockpit. Standing at the tail end of the chopper, I peer into the darkness. The stars in the sky start to disappear as clouds begin to roll in from the south.

"We have six hours before the sun comes up and five miles to reach the backside of the compound. I don't give two shits what we've been instructed. Thor—Tequila, get the women out first.

Preacher and I will search and take out Cortez and his men." He throws his pack on his back. "Agreed?"

"Agreed," me, Thor and Preacher say in unison.

"Turn all your devices off. It's radio silence from here," Cowboy orders as we trek along the tree line.

Almost an hour and a half in, mother nature decides to curse us by letting loose with a rainstorm. Cowboy suddenly throws his fist in the air, halting our steps. Motioning to take cover, we crouch down behind some of the trees, which are becoming less dense the closer we get to the compound. Pointing across the field in front of us in the direction we need to go; I strain my eyes to focus through the heavy rainfall. In the distance, I catch sight of what he sees—faint headlights.

*Shit.*

We huddle closer together. "Double back to the chopper. I don't have a good feeling about this." Cowboy tells us, and we don't question him. Merging further into the tree line, we head back the way we came. With the rain coming down as hard as it is, we can't take the chance of waiting for whoever it is out or risking the possibility it just may be innocent civilians.

Suddenly gunfire breaks out, and bullets shred the bark on the trees around us. Dropping to the ground, we take cover behind a fallen tree nearby. Carefully peering around the log, I catch sight of three men advancing on us. "Three at 2'oclock, twenty yards out."

Nodding, the four of us ready ourselves. Aiming; we fire. "Targets down," I confirm, and we sprint through the trees again, knowing there are probably more of them not far behind. A break in the rain allows us to move faster, and in another fifteen minutes, we breach the tree line and have the barn in our sights.

As we round the rundown barn, an uneasy feeling settles in my gut. I can't confirm why, but something doesn't feel right. A spray of bullets riddles the side of the barn as soon as we jump into the chopper, and I turn the engine over. My heart is racing as I wait for the propellers to gain the momentum needed to get her heavy ass in the air and fly us out of here.

"Fuck!" Preacher yells. "Go! Go! Go!" The side door opens and Cowboy along with Thor lean out and begin firing off shots. Finally, able to take flight, I maneuver the chopper off the ground; gaining altitude, but not before bullets pepper the side. "Shit, man. Where the fuck did, they come from?" Then suddenly, Preacher roars and stumbles back. "I'm hit!" He continues to fire his weapon at the men still shooting at us down below.

My eyes scan what I can see of Preacher as I peer over my right shoulder, then spot blood beginning to soak his pant leg around his left calf.

"Cool your shit and sit the fuck down, Preacher," Cowboy orders, while we continue moving south along the river.

An explosive sound causes my ears to ring, and rattles the chopper, causing my dashboard to light up like a Christmas tree. Assessing everything, I realize my oil pressure, and fuel are dropping fast. "Buckle up, fellas." The engine begins to sputter, and the propeller motors falter. *Shit.* "What the hell was that?" I yell.

"Get us the hell out of here!" Cowboy calls over his shoulder as he crouches down next to Preacher.

"I'm going to have to take us down. Once she loses power, we'll drop like a rock," I warn them. My hands gripping the throttle, I try to find a clearing big enough to land. And just my fucking luck, it starts to rain again, making the situation more complicated.

"You heard the pilot, soldiers. Brace for impact. Tuck your heads and clench those ass cheeks," Cowboy calls out.

In all my career, I've not once had an emergency landing situation due to an unstable aircraft. This being my first, my adrenaline kicks into overdrive. My brothers depend on me to land this hunk of metal safely, and that's what I aim to do.

Surveying my options, I veer to my left, aiming for a small clearing next to the river.

"You got this, Tequila." Cowboy's voice comes through my earpiece. His tone is calm and relaxed as I bring us closer to the ground below. Without incident, I touch the helicopter down just outside what looks to be a tiny farming village and kill the engine.

Sucking in a lung full of air, I close my eyes, before letting all my tension escape me with a heavy sigh of relief. With no time to waste, I unbuckle, toss the headset onto the floor, and maneuver my way into the back of the cabin. "What's the plan?" I ask as we load up with as many weapons and gear we can carry.

"For now, we find some cover." Cowboy tosses my pack to me. "Then, we radio in our coordinates."

"Cover? Where the hell will we find cover?" Thor looks around. Several people living in the village step out of their small homes and notice us standing outside the large ass helicopter sitting in the middle of their cornfield.

"We can take cover over there," I point to a grove of trees. "Whoever shot at us will be here soon. We can't stay here." I quickly add as smoke continues to billow from the undercarriage of the helicopter. "Plus, she's still leaking fuel. We don't want to be anywhere near it if someone starts shooting at us again."

Crossing the field, we decide to keep moving and make our way as far from the wreckage site and small town as we can get. The rain finally let up close to thirty minutes into our walk. "You see that?" I jerk my chin in the direction of a dilapidated shack up ahead.

"Let's check it out," Cowboy announces as we make our approach.

Making sure the perimeter is clear, the four of us walk around the old shack. "It's not much, but it will do for now." Cowboy ushers us inside. "Thor, get to work on that broken radio."

Brushing away a pile of dried leaves with my boot, I kneel on the dirt covered floor. "How much time do you think we have before someone discovers our location?" I slide my pack from my back, unzip the side, and pull out a small bottle of water.

"Not long." Cowboy tucks himself into the shadows keeping watch out of the uncovered doorway.

5

# WICK

Today is the day Everest will officially become a King. The entire club is currently out at Riggs' grandfather's place. Mr. LeBlanc insisted the party be held here. Prez' pop is a kick-ass guy. He doesn't mind the loud music or when things get a bit rowdy; which happens from time to time. At one end of the yard, Josie and Payton are setting up the banquet table and chairs, while on the other side of the backyard Riggs, and his grandfather are preparing the crawfish.

Peering down at my watch, I note the time. "Shit," I mutter under my breath as I scan the yard and spot Fender up on the porch fiddling with his guitar and other music equipment.

Whistling, I call out to him. "Fender!"

Fender looks up and regards me. "What do ya need, brother?" He strolls down the steps, heading in my direction.

"I need to use your cage to make the beer run."

Fender fishes his keys from the front pocket of his jeans and tosses them to me. "No problem, man. You need some help?"

"Naw. You go on and finish settin' your shit up. I'll get Nova to ride with me. He should be here any minute." No sooner do the words leave my mouth, a red car pulls up to the side of the house. Exiting the driver side is Nova's daughter, Piper and climbing out of the passenger seat; a sour looking Nova.

"Are you tryin' to get us killed!" Nova hollers at his daughter's retreating back as she stomps across the yard in my direction. I chuckle at the look on her face. Piper looks ready to spit nails.

"What's got his panties in a bunch this time, sweetheart?"

"Everything," Piper grinds out. "He's driving me insane. He won't even let me drive the speed limit. He sits in the passenger seat, acting like he's going to have a heart attack when I go anywhere over twenty miles per hour."

It takes everything I have not to laugh. These two have been at this driving shit for months. And even though Piper passed her driving test with flying colors, her dad still nags.

"Piper!" Nova shouts as he makes his way in our direction, clearly not finished harping on his daughter.

"Please save me, Malik," she pleads.

I roll my eyes and nod. "Get out of here. I got your back, darlin'."

"Thank you, thank you." Piper kisses my cheek and hugs my neck before she takes off in a jog toward the house.

"Piper. I know you hear me. We're not done talkin'."

Stepping in front of my brother, I stop him in his tracks. "Prez needs us to make a beer run. Come on. We're already late."

"Fine," he huffs, falling into step beside me as we make our way over to Fender's truck.

"Don't think I don't know what your ass just did for Piper there."

"Well, somebody needs to save her from your naggin'."

"I wasn't fuckin naggin'."

I tip my head and give Nova a look. "You're a helicopter dad, Nova."

Nova grunts his response because he knows I'm telling the

truth. Although I get why he is the way he is. Piper is his baby girl. Nova was dealt a shit hand when it came to Piper's mother. She up and fucking bailed the minute Piper was born. I suspect Nova is the way he is with women now due to how shit played out with his ex. Us brothers have been there since the beginning too. Through the diapers, and 2:00 am feedings. We were by his side through every fever, runny nose and earache. We all feel like a bunch of uncles when it comes to that girl. And don't let Nova's man-whore ways fool you. My brother is one hell of a father.

Jumping into the truck, I start the engine, but before I pull out, I turn to Nova. "All bullshittin' aside, man. You've taught Piper well. She's a great fuckin' driver. It's time to loosen the reins and allow her to prove that to you."

"Now you sound like Abel." Nova sighs and scrubs his hand down his face. "She's growin' up too fast, brother."

"Yeah, she is. And there is not a goddamn thing you can do to stop it."

"Fuck." Nova hangs his head, and I can't help but laugh.

"Come on," I clap him on the shoulder. "Let's make this run so we can come back here and celebrate welcoming our new brother."

Nova and I are headed back to Riggs' grandfather's place when out of the blue, he mentions a topic that I'm not interested in engaging in. "You heard from Tequila since she left?"

The muscles in my jaw tick. "No."

"Abel said somethin' about a mission. I was just wondering if she was back yet?"

"And why is that?" I snap.

Nova looks at me, blinks slowly, then a shit-eating grin spreads across the asshole's face.

"No reason. I kind of like havin' her around. She's cool and fuckin' sexy as hell," Nova continues.

My grip on the steering wheel tightens, and the longer he speaks, the more I want to rip his head off.

"I'm thinkin' the next time she's in town, she and I..." Nova doesn't get a chance to finish his last sentence because before I know what comes over me, my foot slams on the brake and the truck skids to a dead stop in the middle of the road.

I ignore the honking of the horns that blare from the vehicles behind me as I turn in the seat to face Nova. "You lay one finger on Vayda, and I will not be responsible for my actions. I don't want you thinkin' about her. Don't even let her name slip past your lips."

By the time I finish spewing my warning, Nova looks delighted with himself. It's then I realize what he did.

"You're a goddamn asshole. You know that?"

"I know," he chuckles. "But it's so much fun gettin' a rise out of you. Plus, it's like pullin' teeth to get you to admit how you feel about Tequila. I don't know who you think you're foolin', brother. We all know."

"What is it you think you know?" I regret the question the second it leaves my mouth.

"That you're in love with her." I don't deny his bold statement as he continues. "You also have it in your fucked-up head; you can't be with her. Even though it's clear she feels the same way." Nova sighs. "I'm going to say this and promise not to bring it up again. You have to let the guilt you're carrying go. Look, my brother hasn't told me the details of what happened with you and what went down with Tequila's brother, Damien, but do you believe he would want you holding on to the past? You were his best friend, and Tequila is his sister. You need to stop and have a heart to heart with your conscience. I guarantee this is not what Damien would have wanted for the two of you."

I let Nova's speech sink in for the rest of the ride back to Mr. LeBlanc's. I can't help but wonder if Nova is right. My problem is not so much what Damien would think about me going after Vayda; it's about me not thinking I'm good enough. The fact is, Vayda is an extraordinary woman; nobody is going to be good enough for her. There is also no man alive who could love her or take care of her as I can.

Back at the house, I park the truck and stay rooted in the driver's seat while Nova hops out. Before he shuts the door, he leaves me a few parting words. "It's time to either piss or get off the pot, Wick. A woman like Tequila is bound to catch someone's eye, and she's not going to wait around on you forever." Nova goes to shut the door but pauses and turns back to me. "Ask yourself this, brother. Can you honestly step aside and let another man be with her? Love her, marry her, and give her children? Tell me, Malik; what do those thoughts do to you?" Without another word, Nova slams the truck door and walks off. I'd be lying if I said his words didn't make my gut clench and blood boil all at the same time.

*Fuck.* The thought of another man taking what's mine has me seeing red. "Shit," I mutter to the empty cab of the truck.

Night has fallen, a fire is burning, the music is low, and laughter fills the air as I sit in a lounge chair while nursing a cold beer. I catch Riggs walking out of his granddad's house and is headed this way with something clutched in his hand. A cut. The one he is about to give Everest. The rest of my brothers and I stand. Everest, who is chatting with Josie, notices the men have gone quiet and a tremendous smile spreads across his face the moment he notices what Prez has. Riggs steps up to where we are gathered and begins his speech.

"Everest, come here, son." Everest sets his beer down on the table beside him and makes his way over to Prez. "Brother." Riggs addresses Everest by the title for the very first time. His chest swells, and he stands a little taller at his President calling him brother. Becoming one of our brothers fills him with pride. I knew early on Everest would make a damn fine addition to the club. "I'm not going to drag this out. You've paid your dues and been a damn good prospect for almost a year now. You've shown the loyalty, grit, and dedication needed to be part of The Kings of Retribution. I speak for all of us as I hand you this cut," Riggs holds the leather jacket out in front of him, displaying The Kings' logo. "We are damn proud to have you wear this patch; representing the club, and proud to call you our brother." Raising our drinks high, the rest of us cheer and salute as he slides on his cut.

A few hours later, I'm back home and standing under the spray of hot water in the shower. The party for Everest ended with Fender passing out on Mr. LeBlanc's porch and the old man leaving him there, after several attempts to wake his ass up. Nova and Piper ended up staying there too whereas Riggs and Luna left the same time I did. Kiwi and Everest wound up going with Josie and Payton back to the clubhouse where I'm sure their party will continue. In all, today was a great day. Now if I could get Nova's words to stop playing out over and over inside my head. Closing my eyes, visions of Vayda's beautiful face push aside all other thoughts inside my brain. Her gorgeous as fuck eyes and how each time she looks at me with her whiskey color orbs. My heart feels like it's going to beat right out of my chest. I love the way her pouty lips part whenever I speak her name. It's as if her name on my lips does to her what her eyes do to me.

With thoughts of Vayda running rampant through my veins, it doesn't take long for my cock to become hard as a rock. Giving in to my desire, I fist my cock in my hand, and begin to stroke. Beads of precum leak from the tip as I start to imagine what the real thing would feel like; what it would be like to have her tight, silky heat milk every drop of come from my cock. "Fuck," I hiss through my teeth, my hand working my dick at an even pace. I haven't been this acquainted with my right hand since I was a teenager but having Vayda hanging around lately has had my dick in a constant state of arousal. I can't count the number of times I'd walk into the clubhouse and smell the all too familiar perfume she wears. My cock would stand at attention every time from the intoxicating scent.

Reaching my left hand out in front of me, I brace my weight against the tiled wall of the shower as the tingling sensation creeps up my spine. Seconds later, my balls draw up before a growl escapes my mouth, and I come.

I take a minute to catch my breath as my release washes down the drain before I cut the water off, climb out of the shower and dry myself off. Snagging the pair of sweatpants I have next to the sink, I pull them on. I'm still absorbed in my conflicting thoughts when I step out of the bathroom and walk past the window in front of my desk when a flicker of light coming from outside catches my eye.

I freeze mid-stride when I notice a dark figure on the other end of that light. *Who the fuck is snooping around my property?* I don't know what the hell is going on, but I'm about to find out. Not wasting time, I grab my pistol and my cell from the table beside my bed and dash out of my room and down the stairs. On the way out of the front door, I place a call to Kiwi since the clubhouse is closer than Riggs' place.

"Yo." Kiwi answers on the second ring.

"I need you at my place—now."

Detecting the urgency in my tone, Kiwi switches from easy going to all business. "You okay, brother?"

"Some motherfucker is snooping around the back end of my property. I want some back-up just in case."

"I'll be there in five," he says, and the line goes dead.

I place my phone on the railing of the porch. With my weapon drawn, I climb down the steps and silently make my way toward the backyard, carefully keeping myself out of sight by hugging my body against the side of the house. Holding my gun out in front of me, I peek around the large shrub that's helping to keep me concealed when suddenly a light flashes in my face, temporarily blinding me. I quickly drop to one knee, all while holding my weapon out in front of me. Not thinking twice about my next move, I fire a single shot at the retreating form that is currently fleeing over the back fence into the woods.

The guy drops to the ground when my bullet hits its mark. In the distance, I hear the rumble of Kiwi's motorcycle as it draws closer. Not waiting on my brother, I take off across the yard, my bare feet snapping twigs along the way. I'm about one hundred feet out from the trespasser when he climbs to his feet. I see the glint of silver two seconds before I hit the ground and three shots are fired in my direction.

"Son of a bitch," I hiss as I start returning fire. Kiwi, who has made his way around the side of the house, pops off several shots of his own.

"Wick!" Kiwi bellows as he runs up to see if I'm okay.

"I'm good, brother." I climb to my feet.

"What in the hell is going on?"

"I don't know. Let's get inside so I can call Prez. And while I'm doing that, you get a hold of the Sheriff. Tell him all is good and to ignore any 911 calls that might have come in. Whatever the fuck just went down here, the club will handle." Kiwi and I make our way back inside my house.

"You think this is some blow back from the Kostas situation?" Kiwi asks.

"As far as I know, we covered our bases with that shit, but you never know. Kostas may have had a farther reach than we thought." Once back inside, Kiwi calls the Sheriff while I place a call to Riggs.

"Brother?" he answers.

"Need ya down at the clubhouse, Prez. I caught someone fuckin' around my house. I called Kiwi to back me up. Shots were fired on both ends before the asshole got away."

"Fuck," Riggs grunts. "You get a good look at him?"

"Naw. Too dark. One of my shots hit him in the leg, though."

"Shit. Meet me down at the clubhouse in fifteen."

I hang up and turn to Kiwi. "Prez is meetin' us at the clubhouse."

Kiwi nods. "Sheriff says two calls were placed to 911, and that he'd take care of it."

"Alright. Let me get dressed, and we'll head out."

Twenty minutes later, my brothers and I are holding church. Riggs slams the gavel, bringing everyone's attention to him. "I appreciate you all draggin' your asses in here so early in the morning. Especially since some of you are still drunk." Prez eyes Fender who looks a little worse for wear.

"As you've heard by now, Wick had an incident at his place. Someone was caught fuckin' around his house. For what? We don't know yet. It could be somethin' to do with Kostas. I know our sources said we didn't have any blowback to worry about, but you can never be too sure. For now, I want you all to stay vigilant." Riggs turns his attention to Kiwi. "Kiwi, I want you to see what more you can dig up on Kostas. See if there's somethin' we missed. Fender, you and Nova take to the streets and see if there has been any talk." With his orders handed out and the guys in agreement as to what to do, Prez slams the gavel, ending church.

Riggs and I stay rooted in our seats while the men file out of the room. When we are the only two left, he speaks. "You stayin' here or going back home?"

Pulling a cigarette from my cut, I light it and take a drag. "I'm fuckin' beat. May as well crash here."

"Good idea. I brought Luna with me. I didn't want to leave her alone, just in case; ya know? I think we'll stay too." Riggs and I are both quiet for a minute before he asks. "You good, brother?"

"Yeah. Just exhausted." I snub my cigarette out and stand. "I'm going to get some shut-eye. I'll catch ya in a few."

Riggs stands and claps me on the back. "Glad you're okay, brother. Take the morning off. I'll open the bar tomorrow."

"Thanks, Prez." I tip my head then stroll my tired ass out of there and upstairs to my room, where I strip out of my clothes before falling into bed. Not two seconds after my head hits the pillow, I'm out.

**6**

# TEQUILA

We sit with our backs against the wall facing the front of the old shack. With the door missing we have an unobstructed view of the edge of the mangrove

separating us from where we landed hours ago.

"Radio working yet?" I ask Thor who has been tinkering with it since we took shelter.

"Negative. Something is scrambling our signal, and cell phone signals are for shit out here." Thor tosses the useless equipment into his gear pack.

"I'm not sure we should stay here much longer," Preacher says, opening a bottle of water.

"The sun will rise soon. It's best if we move at night. The plan is to head east toward the Rio Grande." Cowboy reiterates his plan we discussed earlier. "For now, we wait."

A couple of hours later, I hear a noise off in the distance. "Ssh. Did you hear that?" Keeping low, I move across the floor, and peek out the open doorway. Several vehicles crest the hill, where a road cuts through the mangrove, and at least two jeeps and a truck full of men barrel toward us. With nowhere to run, we prepare ourselves for a fight. "They outnumber us." I ready my rifle as the vehicles flank all sides of the shack, and the men outside surround us.

"Surrender now, and you will not die. Not today anyway," a voice from outside with a thick Spanish accent speaks.

I look to Cowboy, then to Thor and Preacher. We all know we don't have enough ammo to hold them all off. "Scott knows by now something is wrong. I was supposed to report in the moment we had eyes on the compound, and I didn't. Knowing Scott, the wheels have already been put into motion in order to get us out of here. It may take him some time, but he'll come for us." Cowboy sighs and makes a direct order. "We engage in gunfire, we will take some of them down, but we won't win." He makes eye contact with each of us, and we all give him a firm nod.

"We're coming out!" Cowboy yells. "Unarmed." Reluctantly, the four of us drop our weapons to the dirt floor and step outside into the bright morning sun. With our arms above our heads and surrounded by masked men, we surrender. The only visible parts of their faces are eyes, noses and mouths. With no intent on playing nice, several of them rush forward, and rid us of our gear and any remaining weapons they find visible on our bodies, then force us to our knees.

"Who sent you?" someone asks from the right of me.

Turning my head, I make eye contact with a broad, bald man. Pain radiates across my cheek the moment another soldier steps forward striking me with the butt of his rifle.

"Don't fucking look at us, bitch. Keep your eyes on the ground," the masked man spews, as I fall back on my ass from the blow.

"Motherfucker." Cowboy lurches forward, hurtling toward the man who hit me but is stopped by two more men.

"Tie them up and blindfold them as well. We're taking them back to camp," the bald man says, and his men comply.

One by one, they make quick work of binding our hands behind our backs.

"What about this one?" someone asks, but I keep my eyes cast down to avoid another blow. "He appears to be wounded." I hear the click of a weapon, and my heart stops.

"They all stay alive..." There's a short pause before the voice of the bald man finishes, "for now. What we do with them will be up to our superior." Suddenly I feel a presence standing at my side, then hot breath against my ear. "And you pretty thing; if I have my way...I will own you." His voice sends a cold chill down my spine.

Chancing glances toward the rest of the team, I make eye contact with Cowboy, Preacher, and Thor. All of us knew the risks and knew, at some point, a situation like this could happen. At this moment, because it has never happened to me, I can't help being a little scared of what they have in store for us—for me.

Yanked to their feet, I watch the masked men slip woven sacks over each of my brother's heads before the world around me becomes shrouded as a bag is placed over my own head, blocking out most of my sight, and pulled tight around my neck. Roughly groped, I'm ordered to move.

Pulled on, I'm placed in what I believe is the back of one of the trucks, then forced down on my ass. Shortly after, one of the guys falls down beside me. No more than five minutes goes by before men are shouting, the vehicle's engine revs up and we lurch forward.

The heat of the day has increased a good ten degrees in the time we've been riding, which, by guessing, has been nearly an hour now. With the sack over my head, I've lost my bearings and have no idea of which direction we are going. After what feels like another hour, we come to an abrupt stop. My mouth is dry with thirst, and my face is drenched with sweat from the heat and humidity beneath this bag over my head. As we stand still, I try to focus on two men speaking to one another. Their tones are low, and speaking Spanish, but I made out one name spoken. Arturo Cortez. My stomach falls with the mention of his name. We've been captured by the Cartel we've been sent in to take down.

Escorted out of the bed of the truck, they blindly lead us to another unknown location. Wherever we are is out in the open, unhidden by trees, because I can see a bit of the light from the sun filtering through my blindfold. The man whose hold tightens around my arm commands me to move faster, then shoves me forward. After walking a few yards, the palm of someone's hand plants itself between my shoulder blades giving me an unexpected push causing my body to surge forward. Tripping over something, I fall, landing hard on my left side.

The light that had once filtered through the sack obscuring my vision darkens as I hear a door slam shut, then chains against metal, letting me know we are locked inside somewhere.

Silence fills the space around me as I lay still on the dirt floor beneath me until I hear Cowboy whisper. "Tequila."

"I'm okay." I try bringing myself to my knees by tucking my legs under me and uprighting my body.

"Preacher." Cowboy calls out.

"I'm here," he answers, his voice coming from behind me as I rock back, resting my ass on my heels.

"Thor. You still with us?"

"I'm with you, brother," he tells Cowboy.

Suddenly I feel a pair of hands grabbing at the bag over my head, carefully trying to untie the string pulled tight around my neck keeping it in place. "Stay as you are. I've almost got the knot loosened enough to slip it over your head," Cowboy says as he continues to work the knot, then finally pulls the bag off.

The moment I can see, I take in my surroundings. The first person I see is Thor, standing directly in front of me. I look around. We've been thrown into a twenty by twenty concrete cell. No windows; the only light coming from an outside source through the rusted-out holes in the tin ceiling above us. "Let's get those sacks off your heads." Getting to my feet, I take a few steps in Cowboy's direction. "Down on your knees, soldier."

"I feel like you've been waiting a long time to tell me those words." I can hear the grin in his tone, and under the circumstances, I can't help the corners of my mouth turning up in a small smile of my own. Leave it to Cowboy to make light of a situation like this. Once on his knees, I position myself behind him, turn my back, and begin to loosen the knot on the pull string. With my hands still secured behind my back, it's difficult but eventually I manage to undo it and free him from the bag.

Wiping the sweat from his face with his shoulder, Cowboy gets to his feet and faces me. "Shit." He takes a good look at me, and I realize he's referring to my cheek which hasn't stopped throbbing since the prick clocked me earlier.

I shrug. "Take care of Preacher and I'll take Thor." I switch his focus from me to the rest of the team.

Instructing the other two men, Cowboy and I make quick work at freeing them from the bags over their heads as well. "Preacher, how's the leg?" I ask him as he positions himself against the wall behind him, using it to help himself off his knees and onto his ass, stretching his legs out in front of him.

He grimaces as he tries to make himself comfortable. "I'll be alright. It looks like the blood flow has slowed. The butterfly bandage is doing its job—for now." He assesses his injury the best he can just by looking down on it. Preacher is also a field medic. His medical knowledge is vital to the team. "At this point, the one thing I need to be concerned with is an infection," he says.

Cowboy walks the perimeter of the room, searching and inspecting every nook and cranny. Craning his head back, he peers up at the tin roof. "Fuck."

Beads of sweat roll down my face, and the front of my black

tank is soaked from sweating so much it clings to my skin. With no windows, the building they have thrown us in is like a brick oven.

Cowboy straightens his back and rolls his shoulders. "Not going to lie, we've gotten ourselves between a rock and a hard place here. We all know what we need to do, so I'm not going to stand here and lecture you. Staying alive, and keeping our mouths shut is our objective right now." Hearing several men talking from a distance just outside the building, the four of us gather together. Shifting his legs beneath him, Thor brings himself to his feet.

Waiting, we stand rooted in place. "I'm going to go ahead and say it. No matter what they do to me, don't give in." Facing forward, I keep my eyes trained on the metal door. Behind me, Thor takes a sharp breath as if he's about to protest, so I cut him off. "Don't. My life is not more important than any of yours. We are soldiers. I am a soldier." The loud clang of chains sliding against the metal door has us shifting our bodies closer together, preparing for what's to come.

"Stay strong." Cowboy encourages us before the door opens.

The door flings open, and light floods the room. The same man I saw earlier during our capture steps into the doorway. "I see you have removed your blindfolds." His accent is thick, but his English is flawless. "It doesn't matter anymore." Jerking his head, he steps to the side, allowing his men, still hiding their faces, to enter the room. Rifles drawn, they flank our side, herding us out of the building. Though it's sweltering outside, the temperature is a good fifteen degrees lower than it was inside the brick building now behind us. The bald guy walks up, stopping in front of me. His eyes roam my sweat-soaked chest. Defiant, I lift my chin and stare him down. "Ah." He pulls a piece of cloth, tucked in his utility belt, and swipes it across my forehead, dragging it down the side of my face, and along my neck, only stopping when he reaches the valley between my breasts.

"You have spirit." His stare finally connects with mine. He

doesn't say another word. He doesn't have to—his intent is written on his face. And, as strong as I am, my instincts are screaming at me; telling me the man standing in front of me wants to break me. "Take them to bunker C." His hand drops away from my body, but not without letting his fingertips graze my breast along the way before turning and walking away. Turning my head, I swallow hard taking in a deep breath as I try to center my thoughts and control my nerves. Preacher, Cowboy, and Thor are focused on me when I seek them out. All three were wearing the same murderous mask. I give them a reassuring look just before the ends of the rifles are shoved into our sides as we are led across the yard and into an underground bunker.

A cold blast of air hits my damp skin the moment I take the final step and enter the room. I take a good look around. It is significantly larger than where we were located before. Big enough to house many men, yet the space is void of anything but a few pieces of office furniture. To my left, in the corner, I find the source of air coming from a portable air conditioning unit. Forced further inside by the armed men, they direct us to sit on wooden benches that line the wall in the furthest corner of the room. Taking in what is around us, I notice the shackles, several sets of them located on the opposite side of the room, anchored into the concrete.

Without warning, one of the masked men snatches me by my hair, then slams my body against the cold concrete wall, the force hard enough to knock the wind out of me. With my chest against the wall, another unties the rope around my wrists. I cooperate until the bastard runs his disgusting hands over my ass. Throwing my head back, my skull connects with the person standing behind me. A crunching sound followed by explicit Spanish lets me know I broke his nose. My satisfaction is short-lived. My binds fall free, as I'm spun around and punched in the stomach by the one I injured. My body recoils from the pain, and I double over. Just as fast, the two men slam my back against the wall, grab both my wrists, lift them above my head, and clasp the iron cuffs around my already raw skin. Lifting my head, I notice blood dripping from the mask covering the man's face as he stands directly in front of me. Over his shoulder, I take in my comrades as other men hold them at gunpoint.

"I will have you before I watch you die *puta*," he spews.

"Not before I cut your little dick off and shove it straight up your ass." I spit in his face knowing the outcome will not be in my favor. His nostrils flare with rage just before he lands one final blow to my stomach before walking away. Tears sting my eyes from the sharp pain radiating toward the back of my spine.

One by one the rest of the masked men shackles Cowboy, Thor, and Preacher to the same wall. As soon as the men exit the bunker, leaving us alone, Cowboy speaks. "Vayda."

I sigh. Cowboy using my first name lets me know I already fucked up. But, hell, there are some things I can't bring myself to ignore. And being groped is one of them.

"Sugar..." he gives a short pause, "I'm sorry." His voice cracks a bit, and I understand why. I close my eyes waiting for him to say more; maybe tell me we will be okay, or that he won't let anything else happen to me, but he doesn't. He doesn't because we are all in the same predicament. Not one of them can help me as well as I can't help either of them.

Plenty of time goes by before footsteps descend the concrete stairs. Our heads shift to watch a well-dressed man enter the room with an entourage following him. I recognize his face immediately.

*Arturo Cortez.*

His expensive dress shoes slap against the concrete floor as he approaches us. Stopping a few feet in front of Preacher, he walks the line, appraising, until he reaches me. He looks me longer than the others. Grabbing my chin, he rotates my face from side to side, running his thumb across my swollen jawline. "Benito."

"Sir," the bald man steps forward. My eyes shift to him as I put the name to his face.

"Who did this?"

"She was being..." His excuse is cut short when Cortez throws his hand in the air.

"Who?" he demands.

"Mateo, sir." Benito gives up the name of his soldier.

While looking nowhere else but my face, Cortez says without one ounce of humanity. "Kill him."

Again, my eyes shift to the face of Benito. Without hesitating, Benito pulls his weapon from the holster strapped to his thigh, raises his arm, points to another man wearing a mask, and pulls the trigger. For a split second I don't blink, stunned by the coldness of it all, and the fact the man accused not once tried to defend his action or plead for his life, as his knees buckle and his lifeless body falls to the floor.

Cortez continues to stare at me, ignoring the commotion behind him as men carry off their murdered comrade. "Let's begin, shall we?" His lips lift in a sinister grin. "Which one of you is the leader of this unit?" His hands fold behind his back, and his icy eyes finally look away from me.

"I am." Cowboy quickly admits. I want to look at him but catch sight of Benito glaring my way, and my stubborn streak taking over, I narrow my eyes, giving him a go-to-hell look of my own.

"Good. I like the fact that you are taking responsibility for your men." Cortez stops walking, and once again turns his attention to me. "And woman." He continues walking, pacing slowly back and forth in front of us as he pulls a cigar from the inside of his suit jacket. Stopping, one of his men strikes a lighter. Tilting his head back, Cortez blows out a plume of smoke. "Start with the one on the end," he orders his men, and my stomach falls as two of the masked men begin beating on Preacher. "Tell me who you are working for, and I'll end his suffering."

The struggle I feel inside is the same battle I notice written on Cowboy's face as they continue their assault on Preacher.

They are relentless as they beat him with their bare hands; beating him for what feels like forever until a final blow to the side of his head renders him unconscious.

Unfazed and seemingly bored with the outcome, Cortez looks down at the gold watch on his wrist. "Have my wife and child waiting for me when I arrive," he informs Benito as he stands from the corner of the desk he was sitting on as he watched the show. "My apologies for leaving you so soon, but I must join my family for dinner. I hope you take this time to contemplate your future choices. Tomorrow is a new day—a fresh start. For your sake, let's hope you make the right decision." His last words are a warning before he gives a final nod to the men staying in the room, and he takes his leave.

While under the watchful eyes of four armed men, I turn my head while trying to lean forward to catch a glance at Preacher to make sure he's okay.

Being the closest to Preacher, Thor speaks low so that others won't hear our conversation from across the room. "He's still breathing."

Several men carrying large troughs and large amounts of bagged ice enter the room. Racking my brain, I try to put together what is going on until the troughs are slid in front of us, our boots and socks are removed from our feet, and we are instructed to step into them. Welded to the edges are eye hooks. Going down the line, starting with me, they run ropes through the eye hooks and bind each leg to the inside of the tubs. Those bags of ice are then used to fill the containers, covering our feet up to our shins—the final steps taken by pouring a couple of gallons of water over the cubes of ice.

Once every masked man has gone, the lights go out, leaving us in the dark. Sensitive to the cold, I almost immediately begin to shiver, and my skin breaks out in chill bumps. "Shit." I try to ignore the cold.

Moaning echoes through the room. "Preacher?" Cowboy calls out. "Talk to me." We wait a few seconds until we finally hear Preacher's voice.

"God doesn't want me to die today." He's quiet for a minute before chattering. "I'm so fucking cold."

"Listen up. Stay focused." I begin to shiver from the cold, while Cowboy talks. "Preacher, listen to me. Your feet are submerged in an ice bath. We all need to control our movements and breathing. Remember the meditation techniques they teach us to help us fall asleep? Use them. Take your mind somewhere else. Focus on things to block out the cold." Cowboy urges just as sharp pains radiate through my toes.

Closing my eyes, I take a deep breath, hold it in for several seconds, before slowly releasing it. I repeat this step numerous times until time and space becomes a blurred line from the reality I'm currently living in, and one person becomes my anchor.

*Malik.*

I picture his smiling face. The smile I haven't seen in a long time. The one he used to grace me with every time he looked at me. Then I feel his embrace; his lips against mine. The memory is so real I swear I can feel it.

Lost in my head, time drifts away from me, and I no longer feel the bitter cold, causing my body to shiver. Thoughts of Malik become my source of strength and warmth.

A bright flash of light pulls me from my coma-like state, then suddenly light floods the room. Forcing my eyes to focus, I find myself face to face with Benito. "Cortez wishes to see you," he sneers as he pulls a needle out of nowhere.

"If you put one hand on her, you sick fuck..." Thor's words are cut short when another man swings his fist, landing a sharp blow to his ribcage. With a roll of duct tape in his hand, the same guy rips a strip off. One by one, he covers Thor, Preacher, then Cowboy's mouths. Nothing they say or do changes the fact we are about to be separated. That thought alone; not knowing what will happen to them once I'm gone, causes my stomach to clench with trepidation.

"I don't need you fighting me." Benito steps closer, and I flail, trying to avoid the inevitable. "Don't worry; it won't hurt." He flicks the cap off the tip of the needle. "Much." His grin hints at something more before the needle sinks into my skin. Stepping back, he tosses the used needle into a metal trash bin nearby. Watching me, he waits.

Maybe ten minutes later, I can't tell for sure as I've become a little woozy. Benito invades my personal space. Undoing the binds, my body slumps forward across his shoulder. With my body feeling heavy and my brain foggy, I don't put up much of a struggle as he carries me up the stairs and out of the bunker. I do, however, take notice that night has fallen, and realize just how much time has passed since we were captured. As my body sways from side to side as Benito totes me, I listen to his footsteps, hearing gravel crunch beneath his boots. Fighting the effects of whatever drug he injected me with; I do my best to focus. Breathing in and out, I decide to fight. Clasping my hands together in a fist, I raise my arms high, then bring them down as hard as I can, delivering an unexpected blow to his kidney region. Losing his balance, my body slips from his hold, and I fall to the ground. Ignoring the painful landing, I scramble to my knees before quickly getting to my feet, and run.

"Oomph." A heavy weight against my back sends me flying. I catch myself by throwing my hands out in front of me, wincing at the pain as gravel tears at the flesh on my palms. Instinctively, I begin fighting my attacker again. A heavy boot connects with my ribcage, not once but three times, causing me to curl into the fetal position. I'm dragged across the ground, then brought to my feet. With his hands wrapped firmly around my neck, he violently slams my body against a brick wall. Struggling to breathe, I grip his wrist, trying to pry myself free from his hold. Already weakened by the sedative, and in pain from the kicks to my ribs, the fight in me dwindles. His fingers constrict my airway more, and finally my arms fall to my sides.

"Cortez may have taken a liking to you, but I saw you first." Benito's other hand gropes my breast and bile rises in my throat. He squeezes my throat a little tighter. "I plan on taking what I want before Cortez has you." I struggle against him when his hand drops between our bodies and tries to unbutton my pants.

A gun fires, one single shot.

I feel Benito's hand go lax, and his body slumps to the ground.

Dazed by the ringing in my ears from the proximity of the gunshot, and all the blood and oxygen rushing back into my head, I don't see who killed the man at my feet before passing out.

When I wake, I'm lying on my back, staring up at a revolving ceiling fan. I blink a few times. Thirst hits me along with a wave of nausea, which has me rolling onto my side to vomit. A cold rag presses against the back of my neck after emptying the contents of my stomach. Lifting my head, my eyes make contact with a beautiful young woman, sitting in a chair next to the bed that I find myself on. "Where am I?"

The young woman dabs the cold rag across my forehead. "In the home of Arturo Cortez—my husband."

Her admission throws me off, and I stumble back on the bed, but immediately become nauseous and dizzy. Then I think of my team—my friends. How long have I been out of it, and are they still alive? "I need to..." I feel bile rise in my throat again and urge myself to fight the lingering effects of the sedative given to me. "How long have I been unconscious?"

"Hours." The young woman informs me. "He's taken a liking to you," she continues.

Confused, I look at her. "Who?" I scrunch my forehead.

"My husband. And this is not a good thing." Her features harden with the words she speaks as she straightens her back and continues. "I'm willing to help you escape."

"I'm listening," I tell her, still trying to stay focused.

"With one condition." She wrings her hands nervously in her lap. "You take my son and me with you."

# 7

# WICK

I'm acting as a bouncer at Twisted Throttle tonight since Sean called in earlier, saying he wasn't going to be able to make it in. He said something about his daughter's mother and that he needed to deal with her shit. Sean is a good guy. He never calls in, so I told him to handle his business, and I'd take his shift. I like being a hands-on bar owner. I don't do well sitting behind a desk. I enjoy getting my hands dirty and mingling with the regulars. Riggs is behind the bar tonight, and the other men rode in about an hour ago. Kiwi and Fender are playing a game of pool, whereas Nova and his flavor of the night are occupying the table in the back corner. The woman is climbing all over Nova with absolutely no shame. In fact, her ass is on display, and one of her tits is hanging out of the scrap of material she calls a shirt. When my brother catches my stare, I jerk my head in the direction of the hall that leads to the restrooms. Nova gives me a nod as he stands, takes his date by the hand, and guides her toward the back where I know he's about to engage in a quick fuck. My brother gets no judgment from me as long as he takes that shit in private and not out here on the floor for all to see.

"Want a beer?" Riggs asks when I sidle up to the bar.

"Yeah. A shot of whiskey too."

Riggs sets a shot and a cold beer down on the bar in front of me. I place the shot glass to my lips and down the whiskey. Just as I am about to take a swallow of my beer a commotion to my left catches my attention. A young woman who looks to be in her mid twenties has some asshole crowding her and the fucker has a vice grip on her arm. She and her friend have been here for a couple of hours, having a good time and pretty much keeping to themselves. I hang back a second and watch as she politely tries to let the guy down easy; only he doesn't listen. The moment I see her face grimace in pain from the fucker's grip, I come off my stool. Striding up behind the guy, I bring my hand down over his wrist in a chopping motion. My move has him immediately releasing his hold on the woman. The lady gives me a relieved look in the process as her friend who is standing next to her, offers a comforting hug.

"The lady doesn't want to be bothered," I grind out.

The douchebag preppy turns around, his face red and he sneers. "Why don't you mind your own business, asshole." I don't miss the tremble in his voice as he attempts to be a badass. It's all a front. I know I can have pretty boy here pissing in his pants within seconds.

"This is my bar, dickhead. That means when an arrogant, little fucker such as yourself walks into my establishment and tries to strong-arm a beautiful woman into paying you some attention, only to get physical when she turns you down, I make it my business. I also have it in mind to show you some goddamn manners when it comes to females."

"You don't know what you're talking about, man. We were only having a conversation."

I look at the woman he's referring to. "Ma'am. Do you want to talk to this prick?"

She shakes her head. "No. My friend and I came here to celebrate my promotion at work. Alone. I told him that."

"Good for you, darlin'. How about you and your girl head on over to the bar. Tell the bartender Wick said your drinks are on the house tonight." I wink at the two women for good measure just to piss pretty boy off. Both ladies smile at me.

"Thank you."

I watch them walk up to the bar, say something to Riggs then point in my direction. Riggs gives me a nod before he goes about serving the two women. I then turn back to the little shit behind me, who looks like he's ready to spit nails. "Time for you to go."

"Are fucking serious, bro? First, you cockblock me, and now you're kicking me out?"

"First, I'm not your bro. Second, let this be a lesson that no means no, dickhead." I get in the guy's face. When I think the man has had enough and is going to admit defeat by walking away, I catch the slight tick in his jaw as he balls his right fist up at his side. I know what move he's about to make next, and I'm ready for it. I also see this takedown is going to be too easy. Rearing back, the guy brings his fist up and goes to clock me in the face. Dodging his blow, I bring my left arm up to block him at the same time, my right fist lands a solid punch to his gut, making him double over and gasp for air. Next, I fist his hair and bring my knee up, connecting with his face. Blood spurts from the guy's nose, and he yelps in pain as he falls to the floor.

"You broke my nose," he sputters.

The guy flinches when I lean over his battered body and fist the collar of his shirt, bringing him back to his feet. "Let this be a lesson learned you little shit." I drag him toward the door. "I don't want to see you back here." I shove him outside, where he falls to his ass on the ground. Standing on the sidewalk in front of the bar happens to be Chief Richards. Chief looks at the guy I just tossed out, then back at me with a lifted brow.

"Evenin', Malik."

"Evenin', Chief."

"Everything alright here?"

"Yeah. Just takin' out the trash."

Chief Richards grunts and looks down at the man who is still sitting on his ass, looking up at us in shock while holding his bloody nose. "Best go on and get out of here, kid."

Finally doing the smart thing, the guy climbs to his feet and retreats down the street. After I watch him turn the corner out of sight, I bring my attention back to Chief Richards. "What brings you by tonight?"

"Thought I'd stop by on my way home to give you an update on the incident you had at your house the other night."

"You find out who it was?"

"Yeah. Six hours after I got a call from one of your guys, a kid checked into the hospital with a gunshot wound to the leg."

My jaw clenches. "Where is the motherfucker now?"

"He's still in the hospital but is being released in the morning. He'll be turned over to Juvenile Detention."

My head rears back. "He's a minor?"

Chief sighs. "Yeah. The kid is only sixteen. He confessed to two other break-ins in the area. It turns out he's not a bad kid, he just got himself mixed up with the wrong crowd. He's also being raised by a single mother. I met her last night at the hospital. She is beside herself. Had no idea what her son had been up to. I came down to see if you wanted to press charges against him for trespassing."

"Fuck." I shake my head. "Me pressing charges is the last thing the kid and his mom need." I scratch the back of my neck then start to formulate a plan. "See what you can do about the other break-in charges against him. Talk to his mom. Give her Fender's name and number. He's been mentoring a couple of boys down at the youth center. I'll talk with him later and let him know to expect her call."

"Thanks, Dawson. I figured you would do right by the kid. I'll pass your message along to his mother." Chief tips his head and heads back to his patrol car.

Back inside the bar, I take my usual seat at the bar. Riggs sets a fresh beer down in front of me. "What did the Chief want?"

I relay the details of what Chief Richards told me, and Riggs agrees with my decision. "You made the right call, brother."

The next morning everyone is at the clubhouse for breakfast. Josie and Payton are in the kitchen cooking while myself, along with Riggs and his woman Luna, Kiwi, Fender, Nova, and his daughter Piper are sitting outside of the clubhouse. We have a sitting area that faces the river. The whole front side of the clubhouse showcases the industrial look of the city, while the back has been completely transformed. A couple of years ago, Prez tore up the small back parking lot and put down grass. In the far-left corner of the yard still sits the old swing set that once belonged to Piper. The wooden structure holds some sweet memories, and I suspect it's why Nova or any of us other men have yet to tear it down. When I look at Riggs, who is sitting across from me with Luna on his lap and one of his hands on her belly where she is growing their baby, a smile tugs at my lips. It suddenly dawns on me there will be a little one running around the clubhouse soon enough.

"What's that smirk for, brother?" Riggs questions.

"I was just thinkin'. I can't believe you're going to be a dad."

My friend smiles. "I can't fuckin' believe it myself, but I can't wait to meet him or her." Riggs signs as he speaks, so Luna is included in the conversation.

My cell phone rings interrupting my conversation. Pulling it out from the inside pocket of my cut, I look at the screen to see it's Vayda's dad calling me.

"Mr. Wilder?" I answer the phone. The mention of Vayda's father gets Riggs' attention since it's so out of the blue for her dad to be calling this early on a Saturday morning.

"Have you seen the news?" he asks, his tone sounding panicked.

Getting to my feet, I make my way inside the clubhouse with Riggs hot on my heels.

"Talk to me, Sir. What's going on?" My gut clenches in the half second it takes for him to reply.

"My girl is missing, Malik. My baby is missing, and I'm finding out over the goddamn news."

I swear my heart stops the moment he says those words. "Turn on the news!" I bark to no one in particular. It's Fender who turns the TV on. The news anchor's voice fills the clubhouse.

*"We have yet to confirm whether there are any survivors. All we know now is that Captain Vayda Wilder was piloting the aircraft. There is no other word on her and the three-team members she was with. There is also no word on what sort of mission they were on. We will continue with this breaking news coverage and bring you the latest developments as they come in."*

The second the news anchor finishes her story, and the program cuts to a commercial, I head in the direction of the room where the club holds church. "Mr. Wilder, I'm going to hang up and call you right back. I need to call Scott."

No sooner do I hang up with Vayda's dad when the landline on the table in front of me rings. I already know who it is. "Scott. You better have some answers for me."

"I take it you saw the news?"

"That and Vayda's father just called me. Speaking of, can you patch him in?"

"One second." The line goes silent while Scott taps Mr. Wilder in on the conversation. Scott is the mission coordinator for Vayda's current assignment. Riggs and I have worked with him on many occasions. "Look. All I can tell you is I lost communication with Vayda, Burks, Thorstad, and Miller forty-eight hours ago."

"Forty-eight hours?" I bark. "What the fuck, Scott. Why are we just now being informed? Why is this shit all over the news? Vayda's mission is supposed to be classified."

"I've been over here dealing with my superiors, Dawson. I'm breaking protocol by being on the phone with you now."

"Is there any word on if my daughter is alive?" Mr. Wilder questions.

Scott sighs. "Honestly, I don't know. They haven't sent in search and rescue."

I look at Riggs, who is standing over my shoulder. He nods, giving me the signal he's all in. "Scott..." I go to say only to have him cut me off.

"There is a plane waiting for you and LeBlanc. I'll see you both in a couple of hours."

"Is this stunt going to rain fire down on your head?"

"At this point, I don't give a fuck. All that matters now is bringing my team home. Besides, since when have you ever played by the rules, Dawson?"

"Fuckin' never. See you soon."

Scott disconnects, leaving Mr. Wilder and me on the line. He's silent, but I know he's still there. "Bring my baby girl home, Malik."

"You have my word."

It's late afternoon by the time Riggs and I make it to Texas, where an SUV was waiting for us at the airport to take us straight to Scott's house, which also doubles as his headquarters. Scott's estate sits on endless acres of land out here in Texas. It's also where he has a chopper waiting to fly us to Mexico.

Hopping out of the SUV, I jog around to the back, open the

hatch and retrieve my gear. Riggs stands beside me doing the same. When we make it to the chopper and climb in, Scott is sitting in the pilot seat buckling his safety belt. "You get clearance?" I ask.

"Nope. But I don't need it. I have my own connections."

"Good enough for me. Let's roll."

With Scott living so close to the Mexico border, flight time is just over an hour. With my thoughts running rampant, it is going to be the most extended hour of my life. I keep playing different scenarios in my head. Will we find her dead? Is she alive and injured? The third scenario has my gut churning with dread. I know all too well what Vayda's missions entail. Cartels, drug trafficking, and the sex trade. To the Cartel, women are used as nothing more than to make a profit. They are nothing more than expendable property. Once a woman is used up and has served her purpose, she will be tossed out like yesterday's garbage and killed. I close my eyes and clench my fist at the mere notion of what Vayda may very well be enduring at this very moment. Because if she were captured, there would be only one outcome for her in the ways of the Cartel. Hearing Riggs' voice come over my headset, brings me out of my head.

"Don't fuckin' go there, brother. I can tell by the look on your face you're thinkin' the worst. Keep your head on straight. She's going to need you."

"That's if she's still alive."

"Tequila is one of the strongest women I know, Malik. She's a survivor."

I spend the remainder of the flight repeating Riggs' words. Vayda is a survivor.

"We're coming up on where Tequila's emergency landing point would have been." Scott's voice crackles in my ear.

Just as the chopper clears a cliff, I spot it. "There!" I point to my right where Vayda's helicopter wreckage lies in a cornfield.

Instead of landing, Scott circles the area to get a feel of our surroundings.

A compound is located twenty miles from where Vayda landed. Scott informed us this was where Vayda and her team had intended to extract a dozen women held by a man named Arturo Cortez. Not wanting to make our presence known, Scott doubles back in the opposite direction of Cortez's compound. "I'm going to put us down six miles out. We'll have to go on foot to the compound."

"Copy," Riggs and I say at the same time.

By the time we find a secluded place to land, I affirm we only have a few hours before daylight. Right now, the bleak darkness is on our side. Scott, Riggs, and I move through the dense brush in the direction of the wreckage until we come upon the cornfield and Vayda's chopper. I'm the first to reach the aircraft. Riggs is covering my back with his weapon drawn. Pulling a flashlight from my utility belt, I shine the light inside. "There's nobody here."

Using the light, I scour the area around the helicopter, looking for a clue as to what direction Vayda and her team may have gone.

"Over here," Riggs calls out.

When I make it to where Riggs is standing with his flashlight pointed at the ground, I take in the tracks in the dirt leading north towards the mangrove of fruit trees. Following the small road, it leads us to a rundown shack, which we also find to be empty. "Boot prints everywhere."

"You thinkin' they hunkered down here before someone found them—before they were ambushed?" I ask.

Scott nods. "Had to have been. The chopper was empty. And someone was here. Look." He points to the ground. "Tire tracks. If they hadn't been taken, Vayda and the guys would have found a way to contact me by now. The only other scenario is Cortez has them."

"Fuck," I hiss.

"The way I see it," Scott continues, "we have two options here. One, we wait until my backup comes."

I interrupt him. "How long until they get here?"

"Two hours, maybe more."

"Fuck no. I'm not waitin' that long."

"Figured, you'd say that. So, my second option is, the three of us go in guns blazin' and kill every motherfucker who stands in our way and get my team back."

"Option two is the only motherfuckin' one I'm willing to accept," I say vehemently.

"You heard my brother, Scott," Riggs clutches my shoulder. "Let's kill the bastards and bring our family home."

Once we make our way back through the cornfield, we come upon a heavily wooded area and some steep foothills. Not taking any chances, we enter the tree line, keeping off the road leading us to Cortez's compound.

Sometime later, the three of us are lying flat on our bellies just beyond the tree line on the backside of Cortez's house. Looking through my night vision goggles, I case the layout around the compound. Riggs and Scott do the same. "We got one at the back entrance, two on the roof."

"I just clocked one at three o'clock headed east," Riggs whispers.

Swinging my head in that direction, I catch sight of a man making his way toward what looks like a barn. What's odd is the barbed wire fence that surrounds the structure. "How much you want to bet they don't keep stock in there."

"It's not." Scott chimes in. "My intel says that is where Cortez keeps the women."

"You have any information on the layout of this place?" I look at Scott.

"I do. The house is six thousand square feet. When you enter the back entrance there," Scott points straight ahead. "You will be entering the kitchen. To your left is the dining room, and to your right, a study. Once you exit the kitchen, you will walk into the great room. To the left of the great room is a hallway with three bedrooms. To the right is the front entrance of the home and a staircase that leads to two more bedrooms upstairs. Cortez sleeps in the master suite upstairs. My intel also told me that when Cortez had the house built, he also had a two thousand square foot basement built underneath the home. The basement access is through a door between the two bedrooms on the main level. Rumors are he recently had a tunnel built under the house as well, but I can't confirm that bit of intel."

Crawling backwards away from the tree line, I retrieve my pack that is propped against a tree and begin readying myself. Silently Riggs and Scott do the same.

I'm just about to ask the guys our game plan for breaching the house when a shot rings out. I duck behind a tree as a bullet whizzes past my head. "Fuck. We've been made."

To my left, Riggs has taken cover as well, while to my right, Scott has dropped to the ground and has his rifle pressed against his shoulder and his eye on the scope. He fires off two shots. "I'll cover you two. Go!" With Riggs at my back, we take off in the direction of the house the same time four men come charging at us out of nowhere. Aiming, I fire a shot into the head of one man, the same time Riggs takes out another. Just as the other two men raise their weapons, their bodies jerk backward as blood spills from their chest. Scott's voice comes through my earpiece. "Eliminated. I lost two targets on the roof. They ducked out of sight."

"Copy."

When we reach the back entrance, I test the door handle to find it unlocked. Before opening the door, I throw up my arm and give Riggs the signal to cover me. He nods. With my gun aimed, I enter the home. Knowing time is of the essence, I quickly and quietly make my way through the kitchen until we come upon a hallway. It's also where Riggs and I come upon the door that Scott said leads to the basement. My gut churns at what we may find down there, but I look at Riggs and nod. "Cover my six." As soon as I open the basement door, a man appears at the base of the stairs. Finding my mark, I put a bullet in him before he has a chance to blink; his lifeless body slumping to the floor. When I clear the last step, I'm shocked at what I find: Thor and Cowboy shackled to the wall by their wrists. Cowboy currently has a man's head in a vise-like grip between his thighs. "It's about time you fuckers showed up." Cowboy releases his hold on the guy, who falls to the floor dead.

Riggs rushes past me to retrieve the key to the shackles off the dead guy while I crouch down to the cold concrete floor to assess Preacher, or who I assume is Preacher. It's hard to tell with the shape his face is in. The first thing I do: check for a pulse and breathe a sigh of relief when I find one.

Looking over my shoulder, I scour the basement looking for Vayda.

"She's not here," Cowboy informs just as Riggs removes the metal from his wrists, and he makes his way to Preacher's side.

"One of Cortez's men took her a few hours ago."

"Fuck," I hiss.

Suddenly, the ground shakes from an earth-shattering explosion at the same time Scott makes his appearance from the bottom of the basement stairs. He doesn't stop to ask questions or even take the time to absorb seeing his team member lying on the floor nearly lifeless. "Backup has arrived. Dawson, you, and LeBlanc find Wilder. I'm going to get them out of here," Scott says as he hauls Preacher's unconscious body over his shoulder in a fireman's hold, while Cowboy helps Thor from his binds. "I caught sight of Cortez fleeing the compound in a jeep. I have one of my men on him. There was no sight of Wilder with him. That means she must still be on the premises."

Not wasting any time, I exit the basement and go in search of my woman. I don't slow down until I make it to the second level of the home. The first bedroom I come upon; I test the door to find it locked.

"Cover me, brother," Riggs orders just before he uses his shoulder to bust the door open. Inside the bedroom are a queen size bed and a crib. "Clear," I call out.

Next, we make our way to the last door at the end of the hall. I turn the knob and find it locked. This time it is me who breaks the door open, causing the hinges to splinter by using my booted foot. Immediately my eyes zero in on Vayda, who is lying motionless on a bed. Beside her is a young Latino woman who looks to be no older than her mid-twenties. She and a small child are sitting on a chair next to the bed Vayda is in. I keep my gun trained on the woman, not wanting to take any chances. Though if I had to go by the look of sheer panic and fear on her face, she is not a threat. With that thought, I rush to my woman. "Baby." I gently place my hands on her body and roll her toward me. "Son of a bitch, " I grind out when I see the state of her face.

Vayda groans. "Malik."

"Yeah, baby. It's me."

"You're here." Vayda cracks her one good eye open.

"I'll always come for you. Now, come on. Let's get out of here." I reach my hands underneath her body and scoop her up into my arms. "Hold on to me, baby."

Vayda wraps her arms around my neck. "Cowboy, Thor, and Preacher?" she questions.

"They're okay. Scott got them out." I feel some of the tension leave Vayda's body when I tell her that her team is safe.

"Let's get the hell out of here, brother," I say to Riggs as I go to walk past him.

"Wait," Vayda breathes out. "They're coming with us. I promised."

"Who?"

"I think she's talking about the woman and child, brother," Riggs supplies.

I turn back and eye the young woman who is now standing with a little boy clutched to her chest. "Do you speak English?" The woman nods.

"What's your name?"

"Zara."

I don't ask any further questions. I don't need to. If Vayda says this woman and her child are coming, then that's what will happen. "Alright, Zara Let's go."

8

## TEQUILA

Another explosion rattles the walls of the house as Malik keeps a steady pace making his way toward the end of a long hall. My nausea returns with a vengeance as my body rocks in his arms, and I become slightly dizzy.

"Are you okay?" Malik looks at me.

"I may throw up on you," I confess as I breathe in through my nose, trying to let it pass. "Malik, we could move a lot faster if you put me down." The words leave my mouth, even though I feel safe right where I am.

"Not gonna happen, baby." His grip tightens as he jogs down the stairs. "Riggs?" he calls out. Looking behind us, I catch sight of Riggs, who has Zara and her son directly in front of him.

"Right behind you, brother." We pause on the last step, as Malik checks for safety before moving us forward toward the front door. "Scott is in my ear. He secured transport back to the chopper. We have got to move."

Before we reach the door, a bullet whizzes past my head, shattering a large mirror hanging on the wall. Pushing Zara and her child behind him, Riggs aims his rifle, taking out his target.

Catching sight of a second guy, and acting on pure instinct, I reach down, pulling Malik's pistol from the holster, watch the red dot paint the fucker's forehead and pull the trigger.

Riggs' eyes cut to me. "Thanks."

"Where the fuck are you?" Scott's voice can be heard coming from the earpiece in Malik's ear.

"Where are you located?" Riggs asks, peering through the broken window. He looks back at Wick, who is still holding me as if I weigh no more than a feather. "Scott found an unmanned jeep on the west side of the compound."

"I know where he is." Zara's soft voice trembles. "It's where the women are kept." Her eyes cast down to her feet.

"Hey." Riggs grabs Zara's attention, and her face lifts to look at him. "Keep up, and stay between me and Malik." He gestures to himself then to Malik. "Once we exit this house, we don't stop moving until we reach the other side of this compound. No matter what." Riggs' face hardens slightly. "You understand?"

Zara nods. "Sí. I understand." She kisses the forehead of her little son, who has been mute this entire time, but his eyes widen as he sees things no child should ever have to see.

Malik pulls my body closer to his, and his eyes drop to the weapon I still have a firm grip on. "Ready?" The depth of emotion in his eyes catches me off guard, but as always, I recover.

"Ready when you are." My statement holds more meaning than the current situation, and from the way Malik's expression shifts, I realize I have projected my inner feelings. I know—wrong time and place. But I have never hidden my feelings from him, and I'm not about to start now.

Without further discussion amongst us, Riggs opens the door, checks to make sure we are clear to exit. With a simple hand gesture, he covers us as we make a run for it.

As Malik jogs across the property, I keep my eyes trained. Passing several lifeless bodies along the way, before spotting

Scott's location, on the south end of the building Zara said the women are kept. More determined to make sure they get out of this godforsaken place; I start to squirm. "We need to get those women out of there." I push against Malik's chest, wanting him to release me.

"The other team has them secured." Malik lifts his chin as we approach the side of the building. Looking closer, I notice the dead man next to the door, which is open. Finally, he loosens his hold on me and lowers my feet to the ground just as we round the corner where we find Scott waiting for us next to an old cargo truck that looks to be straight out of WWII. "Did you check to see if this old ass hunk of metal runs?" Malik keeps his hand on my waist and guides me to the back end of the vehicle.

"She's old, but she runs." Scott takes a good look at me. By the look on his face, my appearance matches how I feel. He then looks past me. "Who's this?" Turning, I find Zara a couple of feet away, clenching her son.

"No time for introductions. Let's get the fuck out of here," Malik orders.

The second Malik places me in the back of the truck, my eyes land on three familiar faces: Cowboy, Thor, and Preacher. "Fuck, sugar, it's good to see that gorgeous face of yours." Cowboys gets up from his seated position, helping me stabilize myself. Then glances over my shoulder. "I've got her, brother." I realize he's talking to Malik, which I feel is still behind me.

"Miller." Malik acknowledges him with a cold tone to his voice. Looking back at him, I narrow my eyes, giving Malik a look, which he is paying no attention to. No. his eyes are trained on Cowboy. I know the look. It's the same one he uses to run off every man within a hundred feet of me. Now is not the time, I tell myself.

"I need to load you in the truck. To do that, I need you to let me hold the kid." I hear Scott say. Noticing Zara is having a hard time letting one of the men help her; I sink to my knees. Avoiding the sharp and painful pull at my side, I lean forward and hold my arms out.

"Zara." Her head whips in my direction, and I notice right away she is scared to death. I think the reality of her choices is just now hitting her. "I'll hold him," I offer. Without hesitating, she passes her son up to me, and Riggs lifts her off the ground and into the truck, where she settles beside me. Smiling at her, I place her son on her lap. "We'll take care of you. I promise." I assure her as Malik climbs into the back with us.

"You three hunker down near the cab of the truck back there," he tells us.

Sliding our asses across the bed of the truck, we position ourselves in the safest location. The engine in this old piece of shit sputters and comes to life just as gunfire rings out. "Get down!" Malik shouts, and I cover Zara and her boy with my body as Cowboy and Thor form a shield in front of us. The truck lurches forward, and the tires spin as Scott drives us away from the bullets.

Before long, the sound of gunfire fades. When we finally sit up, the only visual left of Cortez's compound is the bright orange glow and flames licking at the night sky from where his house once stood. My attention shifts to Zara. Tears are streaming down her face as she watches the scene slowly disappear as we get further away. I don't know her story, but those don't look like tears filled with sadness. Those are tears of relief.

A hard bump in the road causes me to wince and grunt in pain. I grab at my side. "Let me see." Thor scoots closer. He grabs the hem of my shirt, and I allow him to raise it. "Shit." His fingers lightly press on and around the sensitive area. My breaths shudder when he probes one spot, and I let out a whimper.

"Take your hands off her," Malik warns, and my eyes cut to him.

"You're joking, right?" I'm put off by his attitude at the moment.

"Calm down, brother. It looks like our girl here has some

busted ribs." Thor gives Malik an indifferent look yet stays right where he is. I notice the muscles on Malik's jaw twitch.

"You should have told me." He looks right through Thor like he doesn't exist locking eyes with me.

"Yeah, well. We were in a hurry back there. I'd say we had no time for a rundown of what I've been through." I harden my face when we hit another bump in the road.

"Wilder." Malik tries to come at me by using my last name and a stern stare. So, I level him with one of my own.

"Dawson." I throw right back at him.

Before further words can be exchanged between the two of us, the truck slows to a stop, and Riggs' fist bangs against the cab's rear window. "Roll out." Before Thor can help me to my feet, Malik is at my side. "We should have some compression bandages on board in one of the medic bags." His tone is much softer. With all the adrenaline leaving my body and effects from the drug wearing off more, I'm starting to feel the side effects of the beating I received hours ago. Malik helps me to the edge of the truck and eases me to a sitting position. Jumping down, he helps me out of the truck.

Scott and Riggs are leading Zara and her son to the chopper, while Cowboy and Thor help assist Preacher.

Once we're all aboard, Malik makes quick work of wrapping my ribs. "Are you going to tell me what happened?" He hands me a pain pill and a bottle of water to wash it down.

"Does it matter?" I'm able to ignore the discomfort as his fingertips graze my battered ribs, but I can't control the way my skin prickles with his touch. I look to the other side of the cabin, where the rest of my team sits, thankful that they are alive.

"It matters," Malik whispers, but I don't dare look back at him. After a couple of seconds, he pulls my shirt down over the bandage.

"How's Preacher holding up?" I ask, and Cowboy answers as the rumble of the engine and the propellers begin to spin.

"He'll be okay." Cowboy speaks above the noise. "The important thing is we're all going home—alive." He says all this, but his eyes land and stays fixed on Zara and her son.

With a slight tug, Malik guides me to lean back against him, tucking me carefully into his side. "Relax." His warm breath skates across my skin when he whispers in my ear.

Once in the air, I allow my body to relax and sink further into the warmth of Malik's body. My only thoughts are of home as I drift off to sleep.

Hearing a dull and persistent beeping, I crack my eyes open. After a short flight back to a secured location last night, me and the others were transported to a medical facility, where they looked us over and where they decided to give me a little more medicine to ease the pain. Shifting in the bed, a sharp pain radiates across my ribcage, reminding me of my fractured ribs and the dead man who gave them to me.

"Hey," Malik's voice comes from the left of where I'm laying. Turning my head, I find him sitting in one of those uncomfortable hospital chairs, with his feet propped up on the foot of my hospital bed.

"Hey." I grimace, trying to pull myself up in the bed. "What time is it?" Digging his phone from his pocket, Malik checks the time.

"Almost noon," he tells me and plants his feet on the floor. "You hungry?"

"I could use a strong cup of coffee." Pushing the button on the side of the railing, I raise the head of the bed a bit more. Looking over at the closed window blinds, I mention, "it's still a bit dark outside. I assumed either I haven't been asleep long, or the meds had me asleep most of the day."

Malik stands. "It's storming like crazy outside." Striding across the room, he twists the blinds open, and I take in the dark clouds and gusty wind blowing the tops of the trees. "I'll go grab us a couple of coffees from the cafeteria. I'll let the nurse know you're awake." Malik looks back briefly then exits the room.

Before Malik returns, the nurse enters the room, followed by the doctor who took care of me when I arrived several hours ago. "Miss Wilder, how are you feeling?" He flips through the papers he has clipped to the board in his hand.

"Like someone beat the shit out of me."

His older sharp blue eyes peer at me over his black frame eyeglasses. "Yes, well, other than the three fractured ribs you sustained, your only injuries are to your jaw and your scraped palms. Also your CAT scan came back clear."

"So, does that mean I'm free to go?" I ask him, and Malik walks into the room, holding two coffees.

"Look who I found." He gestures with a smile, and my dad falls beside him.

"Daddy." I beam, grateful to see his face.

He continues to make his way over to the side of my bed. "Pumpkin." He leans down and kisses my forehead. "How are they treating you? They try feeding you some of that shitty hospital food yet?"

"I just woke up," I inform him. My dad brings his hand up from his side, and he is holding a brown paper bag. "I love you, Daddy." I proclaim snatching the bag from his hand, and he chuckles. Reaching inside the bag, I pull out the pastry, still warm, and take a huge bite. "Mmmm. Thanks," I say with my mouth full.

"Apple fritters have always been your favorite, and much better than that nasty fruit jello they try to feed people around here." My dad shivers.

"Well, Miss Wilder. I'll leave you to visit."

No sooner does the doctor leave, Scott walks into the room, accompanied by Cowboy and Thor. "Hey, Darlin." Cowboy steps to the foot of my bed. "How are you doing?"

"I'm good. How's Preacher doing?" I look from him to Scott then Thor.

"He's going to be okay. Preacher has a concussion and a broken collarbone. The staff here is keeping a close watch on him for a few days." Cowboy looks down at his feet then lifts his eyes back to my face. "I'm sorry."

"No one has anything to apologize for," I tell him honestly. "Shit went south. It happens. I know what I signed up for, Travis." I watch him swallow hard; then, he lifts his head.

"Did the son of a bitch touch you?" By the look in his eyes I know what he is referring to. I swear you could hear a pin drop; the room becomes so silent.

"Pumpkin?" My dad steps closer. Behind him, Malik's face has hardened. All of them are staring at me, waiting for me to speak.

Shaking my head, I tell them, "No." A straightforward answer and every man in the room—all my family, instantly relax, and the energy in the room shifts.

"I think you should take some time off," my dad mentions.

Maybe he's right. Perhaps it's time I slow down. Take a break for a while. At least until I've healed. The only thing is, I don't want to go back to my place. "Mind if I come stay with you after they cut me loose from this place?" I ask my dad.

"You can stay with me." Malik quickly interjects himself. He looks at my dad. "That is if you're okay with it." And my father tries hiding a grin.

I look between the two of them and find myself speechless for a moment. "I don't remember asking for anyone's opinion. And I sure as hell don't need you," I glare at Malik, "trying to run my life."

"Not tryin' to run your life, babe. You need someone to look after you while you heal. I've got a big house, and you and I both know the entire club will pitch in if you need them."

I divert my eyes to my dad, who is still suppressing a small grin. You can't see it, but his eyes give his amusement away. "It may be a good idea, Pumpkin. I'm much slower these days. Not that I wouldn't enjoy you being back at home." He rubs the back of his neck. "But I wouldn't be much help. You'd benefit more from staying with Malik."

Malik stands just behind my dad's right shoulder. He folds his arms across his broad chest, with a look of accomplishment on his face, utterly satisfied with himself. Why he wants to keep me close, I don't understand. Having me under his ass all the time for a few weeks is going to test us both more than he realizes.

"I'll feel better knowing Malik will be there if you need him." My dad puts the final nail in the coffin, making the final decision for me with his admission. At least that is what I tell myself; that I'm doing this for my Daddy's peace of mind. Truth be told. I didn't need that hard of a push.

"Okay, Daddy." I give him my answer, and he smiles at me. Even though I can still feel Malik's eyes on me, I don't look back at him.

"I hate to keep you, and I'm due to attend a conference call in an hour. I'll need everyone's official reports on the incident turned in within a week," Scott chimes in, making sure he looks to each of us his comment was directed to. Scott turns, extending his hand to my dad. "Mr. Wilder, it was good seeing you again. You have one hell of a fighter there." Scott looks back over his shoulder at me. "One hell of a soldier."

"Best damn daughter I could ever ask for." Pride shines in my dad's eyes as he says those words, and my heart swells. "Malik," Scott shakes his hand as well. "Take care of her." "Always." Malik nods.

My stomach rumbles, letting me know I still have food in front of me that I would like to eat, and Cowboy chuckles.

"Thor and I are heading out," he says, and I stop him.

"You don't have to go."

"They gave us our discharge papers more than two hours ago.

We've just been hanging around because we weren't leaving until you woke up, and we put eyes on you." Thor steps to the other side of my bed.

"You two going home?" Tearing off a piece of my apple fritter, I pop it into my mouth.

"In a few more days. Thor here is heading home today since he has the furthest to go. I'm hanging back until they release Preacher, then I'm heading home to the ranch," Cowboy informs. Thor bends, kissing the top of my head, and Cowboy comes around the foot doing the same. Some people may see their affection as odd, but we've known one another for a long time, working side by side on many missions. The two of them, along with Preacher, are like brothers to me. They are my family. Chancing a glance at Malik, I take in his expression. One of possession and I roll my eyes.

The two hug my dad and regard Malik before leaving my hospital room. Lying in bed, I finish my meal and drink my coffee while Malik and my dad talk about mundane things like work and fishing. The whole time, Malik stealing glances my way.

There's a knock on the door, followed by a nurse walking into the room, holding papers in her hand. "Miss Wilder, I have your discharge papers. You are free to go home."

# 9

# WICK

Vayda has yet to say a word since we stepped through the door of my house. In all honesty, I don't know what I was thinking about bringing her here. All I knew was I wanted to keep her close to me. I almost lost her, and it was that thought alone that had me making the rash decision she'd be staying at my house. I want to be the one to take care of her. *I'm so fucking gone over this woman.* Seeing Vayda busted up the way she is, understanding what that motherfucker did to her, has unleashed something dark inside me. Something that even I am unfamiliar with. It's the kind of darkness I welcome; one that will wreak havoc on Cortez the moment I get my hands on him. If not for Riggs, I don't know what I would have done when Vayda confessed how she got her injuries. Her battered body carries evidence of where Benito beat her. She told me how she fought him off to keep him from raping her. Thank fuck he didn't succeed. Vayda Wilder is no shrinking violet. She is not one to roll over and accept defeat. Vayda is a fighter. The fact she or any woman would have to fight a man to keep them from taking what he has no right attempting to take, has me seeing red. In my line of work, I have seen what happens to women when men like Cortez brutalize them. Some survive and are able to move on to live somewhat normal lives, while others succumb to the demons that are created, eventually pulling them under. Not that those women are not strong, they just choose to find their peace in a different way. I don't want to think about the kind of woman Vayda would have become had the situation made a different turn. To have the woman in front of me lose her light; to become anything but the amazing human being she is, would have gutted me.

Shaking those unwanted thoughts away, I stop focusing on the what-ifs and come back to the present, where I watch Vayda's eyes scan her surroundings. I don't have to ask if she recognizes what she's looking at. Vayda has never been very good at masking what she's thinking. I know damn well she remembers what she told me all those years ago.

The longer we stand here in the middle of the living room, neither one of us saying anything, the more embarrassed I become. And I'm not one to get embarrassed easily. But really, what kind of person does something like this? Apparently, me. I swear this woman has buried herself deep down in my soul and planted roots there. She doesn't even have to do anything. All it takes is one look, and I'm ruined. It's the very look that has currently taken over her beautiful face. First there was a look of shock, then confusion. It's the last one that does me in. Wonderment.

Vayda continues to walk from the living room to the kitchen, and she stays silent. I know she is not going to mention anything about the house, and neither am I. Truth be told, I wouldn't know what to say. It seems we are both content with my home being the giant elephant in the room... for now.

Vayda clears her throat, breaking the deafening silence. "You just moved in?"

I keep my face expressionless. "No. Been here a few years."

She takes in my kitchen, which is bare—no stools sitting at the island. There is not so much as a fruit bowl on the countertop. Only a small two-person table sits near the large bay window overlooking the backyard. "I stay at the clubhouse more than I do here." I shrug my shoulders.

"Why would you buy such a beautiful house and not make it home?"

Shit. I guess Vayda wants to go there. *Of course, she fucking would.*

I hold Vayda's challenging stare. Not backing down from her interrogation, I reply. "You know why."

My eyes follow the lump in her throat as she swallows. Our eyes stay locked on each other, both in a challenge. We are facing off in a silent battle. When Vayda blinks first then looks away, I know she has omitted defeat on the subject.

Vayda closes her eyes, and her body sways as she takes a deep breath. She's fucking exhausted, and I need to get her to bed. "Come on, baby. Let's get you upstairs." Her eyes snap open when the word 'baby' escapes past my lips. I don't miss the confusion at my using the endearment, but I also don't miss the way her eyes heat every time I use it. The first time I called her that, it was a slip of the tongue. Now, it's because I like the way it sounds rolling off my tongue and most of all, I love the way she looks at me when I say it.

I'm also confusing her by sending mixed signals. Hell, I'm confusing myself. No matter how much I tell myself, I need to stay away, I can't fucking do it. Everything about this situation is fucked up. I have been telling myself for years to stay away from this woman, that I am no good for her, but God help me, I no longer have the strength. Almost losing Vayda awakened a part of me I have kept buried for so long. The part of me that has been fighting the pull we have for each other. Vayda has no qualms about showing me how she feels. It's time I do the same. The only question is, can I get out of my own head to be the man she deserves. Because I can't help but wonder if she knew the truth about the day Damien died, could she forgive me?

With my focus on the woman in front of me, the one who looks dead on her feet and about two seconds away from passing out, I move toward her. In two strides, I came to stand in front of Vayda. I don't ask permission, and there is no warning before I scoop her into my arms, careful not to hurt her ribs.

Vayda gasps. "Malik, what are you doing?"

"I'm taking you upstairs to rest before you faceplant on my kitchen floor." I begin to make my way out of the kitchen and up the stairs. Vayda tries to wiggle her way out of my arms.

"Malik put me down. I can walk."

I stop at my bedroom door and level her with a look that has her halting her movements. "I know you're a tough woman, Vayda. Hell, anyone who knows you, knows you're a badass. That's not something you let people forget, either." Her lip twitches.

"But right now, you're going to give me this. You're going to pocket your tough exterior and your independence and let me take care of you." I swallow the lump in my throat. "I could have fuckin' lost you." The last part comes out harsher than intended. Vayda is a bit taken aback by my tone, but relaxes in my arms and nods.

When I walk into my bedroom, I carry her straight to my king size bed and lay her down. Her exhaustion shows when her body melts into the blanket, and she lets out a heavy sigh as her head hits the pillow. I don't miss the way she turns her head and inhales my scent that lingers where she lays. When her eyes open they lock on mine. Vayda's eyes leave mine, traveling south, and there is no hiding the hard-on currently pressed against the zipper of my jeans. When she sees my noticeable erection, her gaze lingers a moment before sliding back up to my face. This time I am the first to break the silence. "I got to meet the guys at the clubhouse.

There is some shit we need to sort out, one being that woman we brought with us and her kid."

Vayda nods, her eyes getting heavier.

"I'll be back in a while. Josie will be stopping by with your medicine, some clothes and food. She is going to stay with you until I get back. She has a key to the house and the alarm code, so you don't have to get up."

At my last statement, Vayda's posture goes rigid, and her eyes flare. "I don't need one of your club girls to take care of me," she snaps.

It's stupid of me to do so, yet I can't help but grin at Vayda's jealousy. My grin turns into a full-fledged smile when she continues.

"On second thought, I don't think I want to stay here if you're going to have women coming and going all day."

"Josie is not my woman. Her job is to tend to the brothers and help out any way we ask. She also doesn't have access to my home twenty-four-seven. Today is an exception. When Josie heard about what happened she insisted on helping out."

Vayda clenches her teeth. "Whatever."

Losing my smile, my face goes soft. "Get some rest, baby."

Just before I walk out of the room, I stop at the door and look over my shoulder. "Just so you know, I haven't been with any woman in months." I don't wait for a reply. I walk out of the bedroom, down the stairs and to the foyer where I set the alarm. Before climbing on my bike, I fire off a quick text to Josie letting her know Vayda is resting and to let her sleep when she gets here. Josie texts back immediately saying she's leaving the grocery store now and will be here in ten minutes. Payton and Josie are great girls and they are easy to get along with. They are also not catty or territorial over us brothers. They know their place with the club and have no problems with the dynamics of how things work. I wasn't lying when I told Vayda I haven't touched a woman in months. Vayda will see for herself neither Josie nor Payton are a threat. I have no doubt the girls' charm will shine through, and they will all become friends. Hell, Luna was stand-offish at first when she first arrived at the club and met the girls, but now they are the best of friends. Josie and Payton are as loyal to the Old Ladies as they are us men.

Entering the clubhouse, I find my brothers scattered throughout the room. Riggs nods from where he's rooted on a stool at the bar. "You get Tequila squared away?"

"Yeah, brother. She's settled."

"She still givin' you a hard time?"

I sidle up to the bar next to Riggs. "Naw. She was too tired. We'll see how things go once she's had some rest."

"I talked with Josie earlier. She said she was runnin' some errands for you, and then she was going to sit with Tequila while you are gone." Riggs gives me an 'are you crazy' look. "You tell Tequila she was comin'?"

I take a cigarette from the inside of my cut and light it. "Yep."

Riggs chuckles. "I don't imagine that went over well. Not with the death glares thrown your way anytime you so much as stand within arm's reach of one of the girls." Riggs claps me on the back and chuckles. "Good luck with Tequila not ripping your balls off."

"Thanks," I say dryly. "I'm going to need it." I take one final drag of my cigarette before snubbing it out.

"Alright!" Riggs bellows standing from his seat. "I'm callin' church."

One by one my brothers and I follow our Prez into church. The moment the door slams shut; he slams the gavel. "First things first. I know you all have been clued in on what happened in Mexico with Tequila. Her mission was compromised, and she along with her team were captured by Cortez. You also know, that son of a bitch got away. It fuckin' sucks, but our main concern was getting

Tequila and her team out, which is exactly what we did." "How is she?" Nova asks.

"She's banged up pretty good. Got some busted ribs, and Cortez's man did a number to her face. But you all know Tequila. She's strong as fuck and will get through this. She's resting out at Wick's for the time being," Riggs supplies.

Nova regards me from across the table. "You or your woman need something, brother; I'm there."

I nod. "I appreciate that, brother."

A chorus of murmurs comes from all the brothers offering the same. It comes as no surprise my brothers have Vayda's back. I also don't react when Nova calls Vayda my woman. None of the other brothers blink an eye at it either.

"Any word on, Preacher?" I cut in, turning my attention back to Riggs.

"Scott called an hour ago. He will be discharged by the end of the week and headed home to finish recovering."

"What about this Cortez fella?" This comes from Fender. "Any word on where he's hiding?"

Riggs shakes his head. "Nothing yet. As soon as we finish here, I'm going to talk to our guest. See if she knows where he may be hiding and how she fits in with everything."

"Right now, we don't know jack shit about the woman. Only that Vayda insisted we bring her with us," I supply. "And you all know she must have a good reason for asking that of us." My brother nods in agreement.

I turn my attention back to Riggs. "So, Prez. What's the plan? I have to say Cortez still on the loose is not settin' well with me. My gut is tellin' me we need to watch our backs."

"I'm with you, brother. Not only did we invade his home, we also fucked with his operation. Men like Cortez don't go quietly into the night. Retaliation is something we need to be vigilant about."

Prez regards Kiwi. "Kiwi, see what you can dig up about who may have leaked the details of Tequila's mission to the media, and see if there is a connection between that and Cortez knowing as well. Something tells me the person who did is not a threat but an ally. Had it not been for the leak, we might not have made it to Tequila in time."

"You got it, Prez. I'll get with Scott and see what he's been able to find out so far."

Riggs turns to me. "You want one of the brothers out at your house to help keep an eye on things while Tequila is stayin' there?"

I shake my head. "I'm good, Prez."

Riggs gives me a hard stare. "Alright, brother. But at the first sight of trouble, I want both your asses back at the clubhouse."

With those final words, Riggs slams the gavel ending church. "Wick, you come with me to talk to the girl."

Striding into the main room of the clubhouse with Riggs, I spot the woman in question sitting on the sofa watching her son play with Payton on the floor. I take a seat in a chair across from her and Riggs sits in the other. The young woman is fucking terrified as she takes in the two men sitting across from her. With a low tone I try to calm her. "We're not going to hurt you. We only want to talk."

The woman darts her eyes back and forth between me and Riggs while wringing her hands in her lap. "O...Okay. What do you want to know?"

"First, is Zara your real name?" Riggs prompts.

"Yes. My name is Zara and my sons name is Julian."

"Okay, Zara. What can you tell us about Cortez?"

Zara takes a deep breath. "He got away, didn't he?"

"Yes," I tell her truthfully. "Do you think he will retaliate? Will he come looking for you?"

"H...He couldn't care less about what happens to me, but my

husband will come for his son." Zara darts her eyes over to the corner of the room where her son is playing with Payton.

"Fuck!" I bite out, causing the fragile woman to jump. Riggs sends me a warning look to reign my temper in, which I'm finding hard to do at the moment, considering we just found out the son of the man who captured my woman is sitting right in front of us.

"Are you going to send me and my son back to him?" Zara asks. This time I'm the one who jumps in.

"Fuck no. I know you don't know or have any reason to trust us, but we are not the kind of men who will turn over an innocent woman and child to a lowlife like Cortez."

Riggs is the next to cut in. "Vayda promised you protection, and seeing as Vayda means something to the club, you and your son are now under the protection of The Kings."

At Riggs' declaration, I watch as an immense amount of relief pours off the woman in front of us. She really thought we'd turn her and her child over in order to save our own asses. Fuck that shit. The Kings back down to no one. Cortez better bring everything he has to the battlefield because when he faces off with me, he's going to need a whole fucking army.

**10**

# TEQUILA

This is ridiculous." Huffing my frustration, I lean back, letting my upper body and head sink into the mound of pillows behind me. Finally, taking in Malik's bedroom, I realize it's almost as sparse as the rest of the house. Aside from the sizable King-sized bed, which feels like heaven compared to the hospital bed, there's a long dresser with a TV hanging above it and an oversized chair positioned by one of the windows along with a desk on the opposite side of the room.

Bringing my hand up, I cover up a yawn. I can't remember the last time I felt so tired. Not just physically, but mentally as well. Looking over at the nightstand, I spot the TV remote. I also notice the picture frame sitting right beside it and pick it up. My fingertips trace the surface of the photograph as I study the three familiar faces staring back at me—much younger versions of me, my brother, and Malik. Emotions swell, causing my chest to feel heavy. My tired eyes well up, and a few tears stream down my cheeks. I remember the day this photo was taken like it was yesterday. It was the night of homecoming. I was so excited to go. Especially since my dad was set against me dating for so long.

The rule was, I had to wait until high school. So, when I was asked my freshman year by Terrance Johnson to homecoming, I was more than ready to spread my wings. Daddy, on the other hand, wasn't as prepared as he thought he was. I laugh to myself and wipe the tears from my eyes. Most girls go shopping with their moms or girlfriends; I had my Dad. My mood lightens, and I smile. We spent the entire day together. He took me shopping, spending countless hours waiting for me as I tried on dress after dress until I found the right one. To top it all off, he took me to dinner, just me and him, where he gave me a spa day gift card, which I used the day before the dance to get my hair and nails done.

Continuing to stare at the photo, I hone in on the smiles we were all wearing and take in how happy we were despite the little fact none of that night went the way it was planned but exactly how it was supposed to be. My date ended up with a terrible case of food poisoning the night before the dance. Nevertheless, I had a dress, the perfect pair of shoes, and my hair was on point. I wasn't going to let anything stop me. The next day, I put myself together, determined to take myself to the dance.

When I got downstairs, Malik and my brother were standing in the living room with Daddy. My brother dressed in a suit, and Malik sans a suit jacket, staring at me in a way he never had before. I remember the heat I felt from it.

My eyes grow heavy. I set the picture frame back in its place, retrieve the TV remote and turned on the TV. I find it much easier to fall asleep with background noise and sinking further into the pillows. I finally give in to my fatigue. Closing my eyes, I fall asleep.

*Rounding the corner, I step into the living room. There standing beside my dad is Malik, next to him, my brother. "What are you two doing here?" I stop, waiting for someone to answer me as the three men in my life do nothing but stare at me. I start to feel unsure and uneasy, the longer they stay silent. "What?" I look down at myself, thinking something is wrong with my attire. "Do I not look okay? Is something stuck on my butt or something?" I ask as I turn my back to them.*

*My Daddy walks across the room. Grabbing my hand, he twirls me, and I giggle like a little girl. "You look absolutely beautiful, baby girl." I look up, and his eyes are a bit misty. "You look so much like your mother."*

*I smile. I never had the chance to know my mom, but dad keeps pictures of her everywhere. She passed away hours after giving birth to me from a pulmonary embolism. My dad raised us by himself. Being a single dad hasn't always been easy for him, especially trying to raise a teenage daughter, but I've never wanted for anything. I couldn't ask for a better dad. "Thanks, Daddy." I throw my arms around his waist, hugging him. "The girls will be here any minute to pick me up. We haven't discussed curfew yet." I take a step back.*

*"Your friends will meet you at the dance." My brother and Malik stroll in our direction, joining us.*

*"What are you talking about?" I ask, confused. I just talked to Jessica an hour ago. As far as I know, plans haven't changed. Suddenly my stomach sinks to the floor.*

*"I'm taking you to homecoming," Malik rushes to say, and my eyes connect with his. The intensity in them throws me off. He stares at me like I'm prey—like I'm his, and it feels like a fire consumes me. "I mean, your brother and me." He soon adds, causing the spell he had over me to break. My Daddy's shoulders shake with a chuckle.*

*"Let me get this straight." I start to feel a little peeved. "You three," I eyeball all of them, "have decided to take it upon yourselves to change my plans for me?" I raise my brow. "I don't need anyone feeling sorry for me. It's not like I was stood up. Terrance got sick. I'm fine with going solo." I fold my arms, determined to let them see I can stand on my own.*

*"Baby girl," my dad says, his tone telling me to turn the dial back on my stubbornness.*

*I cut my eyes to Malik, who is still focused on me, then my brother.*

"Come on. We'll all have a good time. Promise," Damien says.

"Fine." I give, and my dad grasps my shoulders as he kisses my forehead. "You three have fun." Then he turns toward Malik as my brother heads for the front door. "Take care of my baby girl. Make sure she's home by 10:00 pm." He grills Malik as if he's my date.

"Daddy. It's Friday and homecoming. Come on, can't you stretch curfew just for tonight? Say, midnight?" I give him a pleading look.

"Tonight only." He faces Malik, "You have my daughter home, inside this house at midnight, sharp."

Malik's face turns serious. "Yes, sir." My dad gives him a sharp nod.

"Let's get going, you two," Damien calls from the front door.

Hugging my dad's neck, I retrieve my purse and walk out the door, following my brother and Malik one step behind. As much as I try to hide it, I can't contain my enthusiasm or the way I feel when Malik's palm touches the small of my back before reaching in front of me to open my brother's car door.

Looking back at him, I smile, and he returns one of his own.

Later that night, Malik drives us home. I sit in the passenger seat, tapping my bare toes to the rhythm of the music from the radio, on the floorboard. Meanwhile, my brother is in the backseat, sleeping off the alcohol he and some of his other teammates snuck into the dance tonight. I look in the backseat and laugh when he mumbles in his sleep. "If our dad sees him like this..." I don't finish my thoughts before Malik says, "Don't worry. He won't. Damien is staying with me tonight."

"You're a good friend."

Malik laughs, and it brings a smile to my face. "I don't know about that, but he's the best friend I've ever had. You both are." Those last words, him calling me his friend suddenly doesn't sit right with me. It almost feels like he punched me in the stomach.

"You okay?" Malik looks over at me as he's pulling my brother's car into the driveway of our home.

I swallow the lump in my throat. "Huh?" I look over at him, and he's staring hard at me. "Yeah, I'm fine." I lie. The truth is, I'm feeling a lot of *things at the moment, and I can't process any of them being this close to him. Flinging the car door open, I pick my heels up off the floorboard. With them and my purse clutched in my hands, I take off in a hurry toward the front door.*

*"Vayda." Suddenly Malik is right behind me, and I pause with my hand on the door handle. "Wait."*

*My shoulders sag. Turning, I face him. Why do I feel so awkward? This is Malik for crying out loud. My brother's best friend. My friend. "Thanks for taking me to the dance tonight. I had a great time with you." I pause for a split second before adding, "and my brother." I nervously twist the leather straps of my heels in my hands. Butterflies fill my stomach when Malik brushes my hair from my face.*

*"I forgot to tell you earlier; you look beautiful tonight, Vayda." His eyes fall to my lips, and I think he is about to kiss me.*

*A magnetic force is pulling me toward him.*

*It's the moment everything changes. That's when I know. My entire perception of Malik shifts. Not that I've never noticed how attractive he is.*

*My heart drums against my chest. I want him to kiss me.*

My eyes pop open on a gasp with my heart pounding just as hard as it was while I was lost in my dream. Squeezing my eyes shut, I slow my breathing and shake off the lingering effects.

"Hello? Vayda?" I hear Josie's voice echo through the empty house.

"Great," I mumble to myself. Sitting up, I swing my legs over the edge of the bed. Still agitated that Malik would send Josie over to help me out while he's at the clubhouse dealing with club business, I slowly stand and shuffle across the bedroom and out the door. Before I come to the end of the hall, Josie appears.

"Oh, there you are." She smiles at me. "Were you sleeping?" She takes in my appearance. "Um, would you like something to eat?" She points her thumb over her shoulder. "I bought a few things to stock Wick's fridge and a few pans to cook in. I can fix you something." At the mention of food, my stomach growls. "I'll take that as a yes," Josie giggles. "Do you need help getting down the stairs?" she asks, and I'm quick in rejecting her offer, my words sharp when I say them.

"I don't need your help." I watch her face fall with the bite of my words. She forces a smile.

"Okay. Well, I'll be in the kitchen if you need me." She turns to leave, looking back one more time as I stay motionless before she descends the stairs.

Sighing and feeling a little bad for being such a bitch, I slowly make my way down the stairs, the pain in my side pinching with every step I take as I find my way to the kitchen. *Who does Malik think he is anyway? I'm a grown-ass woman. I don't require a damn babysitter, especially a woman he seems to be cozy with.* Anger bubbles inside me, as I walk into the kitchen, past Josie, ignoring her while I sink down onto the chair at the kitchen table.

"I've never slept with him." Josie says with her back to me as the smell of onions and peppers fill the room.

"What does that have to do with me?"

"More than you want to admit." I watch as she cracks open a few eggs, whisks them in a bowl with a fork, then pours them in the pan. "Wick and I are only friends. It's been that way since I joined the club. I've never warmed his bed." Grabbing a couple of plates from the cabinet, she plates some food, then walks in my direction. Setting the plate in front of me, she settles in the chair across from me. I stare at the food she prepared. "He's a good man, Vayda." She pauses. "Can I call you Vayda, or should I call you Tequila like the guys do?"

I pick up my fork. "Vayda is fine. Listen," I look at her as she lifts a bite of food to her mouth. "I'm sorry about before. I appreciate the help. I do. It's just..." I don't finish my sentence.

"He only wants one woman, and that woman is you. Never seen a man so hungry for another person like he is for you, Vayda."

I let her admission sink in for a moment. "This is really good." I compliment her on her cooking, mostly to deflect any further talk of Malik. Judging by the smirk on her face, she's on to my game and goes with the flow of the conversation.

"Thanks. I'm not the best cook in the world, but I can fix a mean omelet."

The two of us fall silent for a few minutes. "So, how did becoming one of The Kings' club girls come about?" I ask out of curiosity, and she laughs. "Feel free to tell me it's none of my damn business." Finished with my meal, Josie stands, taking our empty plates to the sink.

"I don't mind. I find your forwardness refreshing. You keep it real. More people should unapologetically be themselves like you." She walks back to the table with two glasses of sweet tea, sitting one in front of me. "MC life is familiar. I grew up around a bunch of bikers, Tartarus MC, from North Carolina." She takes a sip of her tea. "I can remember my mom hanging around them as early as when I was two years old." Josie taps the side of her glass with her black painted nails. "As I grew older, I felt stuck, like I was suffocating. Not that I didn't have a good relationship with my second family, I just wanted to go out and see what the world had to offer beyond Blowing Rock."

"So, you left," I state.

"Yep. I supported myself for over a year by singing at biker bars and lending a hand behind the bar when needed. Then I wandered into New Orleans." Josie's face lights up. "I fell in love with the city and the people in it. Riggs offered me a job one night after a gig at the Twisted Throttle, singing and waitressing."

Knowing how MC members can be about other clubs, I ask, "How did your mom, and the MC you grew up around feel about your association with the Kings?"

"To tell you the truth, they were okay with it. Reputation and respect go a long way in the MC world, and The Kings are much like Tartarus in many respects."

"Your mom was okay with you sleeping with men—with being someone else's property?" I ask.

"I know what you're thinking, but it's not like that. I'm not King's property. Not like that. And I don't sleep with all the men. I've only actually slept with Nova and Fender. That's another reason I like it here. They respect women. Who we do, and what we do is our choice. Not all clubs work the same way The Kings do. Riggs only gave me the opportunity after I approached him. And it wasn't until after hearing my story and who I've been associated with in my past that he said okay and took me on. My mom, for many reasons, doesn't like my choices, but it's my life."

"I misjudged you, Josie."

She waves her hand dismissively. "Don't worry about it."

"No. I know how to own my shit, and I let my jealousy get the better of me."

"I appreciate the apology," she nods, then adds, "I respect you a lot, Vayda, and I've enjoyed hanging with you today." Josie smiles.

"I've enjoyed it too." Using the table to help me, I stand. "My entire body hurts like hell; I think I might soak in the tub for a while." Josie stands as well.

"You need any help? I don't mind."

"A little help would be nice," I admit.

Josie strides across the kitchen and lifts a plastic bag from the counter. "I bought you a few things: Shampoo, body wash, toothbrush, things like that. I'll go upstairs and run you a bath, and put all this away." She raises the bag in her hand. "Take your time. If you need help getting up the stairs, let me know?" She says the last part as a question, still sounding a little unsure how she should approach me.

"If I need help, I promise to ask," I assure her.

After watching Josie disappear, I decided to explore the house before heading upstairs. Taking my time, I venture into every room on the first floor. All of the rooms are bare-boned. There is no life in the house—no personal touches of any kind. I still can't get past his home being the spitting image of my childhood dream house, right down to the color of the shutters on the front windows.

"Vayda," Josie calls to me from upstairs. "Your bath is ready."

"Be there in a minute!" I shout, my voice echoing through the empty home.

Once upstairs, I find Josie stepping out of the en suite. "You have a clean towel on the rack next to the tub." She walks to the bedroom door. "Oh, and I laid out some pajamas on the dresser. I wasn't sure what you liked to wear so—anyway, I've texted Wick. He said to tell you he will be home soon." Josie turns to leave.

"Thanks again, Josie."

Her smile is infectious, causing me to smile in return. "No problem."

Waiting until I hear Josie leave, I step into the bathroom, finding the large tub filled with soap suds, and smelling like honey and vanilla. Off to the side, next to the tub, Josie even lit a candle. Slipping off my sweats was easy. Slowly pulling my tank over my head was painful, but removing the support tape from my skin over my ribcage proved to be impossible. That shit wasn't coming off. Leaving it, I lift one foot over the edge of the tub, then the other, before carefully lowering myself into the warm water. The instant my body is submerged, and the heat begins to penetrate my muscles, I sigh. "Oh my god." Leaning my head back, I close my eyes.

A light tap on the bathroom door causes my eyes to pop open and my body to flinch, making the now lukewarm suds-free water slosh. "Vayda."

"Yeah?" I slide myself up. I must have dozed off. Using the sides of the tub as my leverage, I attempt to get out of the tub before the water turns colder, but quickly realize it was much more comfortable getting in than getting out. My broken ribs scream in protest as I try it a second time. "Fuck!" I yell when I realize I might need help. Before I can say anything, Wick bursts through the bathroom door.

"What's wrong?" he pauses when he realizes I'm entirely naked.

"I kind of need a little help getting out of the tub," I admit and regret not thinking ahead and asking Josie to stay a bit longer. With my breasts pressed against the inside wall of the tub, I look at Wick. I watch the corner of his lips twitch.

"You okay with me helping you?"

"You asking yourself that question?" I challenge, but he doesn't budge. "I can't stay here all night, and it hurts too much for me to do it on my own."

Without further discussion, Malik crosses the space between us, bends over, and scoops me from the water. Setting me on my feet, he quickly snags a towel from the rack, wrapping it around my body. "You got it from here?" he asks with worry.

Holding the towel closed, I admit, "Could you help with one more thing?" Malik's eyes deepen with desire. I drop one side of my towel, exposing my body to him. "I couldn't remove the old tape, so I thought soaking in the water may help."

"Come here." He guides me into the bedroom. Grabbing the new sports tape the doctor sent home with me; Malik sits on the edge of the bed. "Cross your arm over your chest for me." Doing as he asks, I raise my arm. Holding the towel to my front, leaving the rest of my body exposed to Malik, he begins to peel the tape from my skin. He's gentle when he does it. Working his way up, he starts to remove the bandage closest to my breast, and ever so slightly, his fingertips graze the side of my breast, causing my body to shiver, and my nipples to harden against the terry cloth towel.

"Breathe, baby." The carnal tone in Malik's voice reverberates through my body, making his simple act of taking care of me feel erotic. The more his fingers caress my skin, the more the ache grows between my legs until I'm throbbing with need. "Done." He stands, and my eyes drop to the bulge in his jeans. "Vayda," I hear the warning in his voice, and I lift my eyes to his. "Get dressed." I open my mouth to say something sassy, but he cuts me off. "Don't." Against my natural tendencies, I keep my mouth shut as he walks out the door, closing it behind him.

Standing in the room, alone, my body raging with sexual tension, I decide to do the only thing I can think of to relieve the ache between my legs. Laying back on the bed, I toss the towel wrapped around my body to the side. Ignoring the pain in my ribs, I reach my hand between my legs to find my center drenched. I can't help the moan that escapes my mouth when the tips of my fingers brush over the top of my swollen clit. Closing my eyes, visions of Malik take over my senses and I imagine what it would be like to have his strong body covering mine while thrusting his cock in and out of me. "Oh, god." I gasp and my pussy clenches at the mere thought of Malik's cock filling me. With my wicked desires driving me to the edge, I give into the pleasure as my fingers continue to work the little bundle of nerves between my thighs until I come fast and hard.

Feeling drained, mentally, and physically, I crawl beneath the warm covers and fall asleep.

Hearing water running, I crack my eyes open, finding the room darkened by nightfall; the only glimmer of light coming from the bathroom door that is partially open. Rubbing the sleep from my eyes, I prop myself up in bed, with my back against the headboard. A moan catches my attention. Catching movement from the bathroom, I lean to the left a little. I now have a clear view through the glass door of the shower where I see Malik's muscular, 6 foot 3 inch frame standing in the tub, with his head hung low as the water cascades over his back. My eyes travel the length of his toned body. When he twists, I catch a glimpse of The Kings' logo tattooed across his back before noticing the shrapnel scars spanning the side of his ribcage and down his hip. Finally, my eyes settle on his impressive cock. Long and thick. My breathing picks up, and even though I know I should look away I can't. The moment Malik fists his cock, I gasp.

# 11

# WICK

I could hear Vayda's gasp through the hot water currently pelting down on my back. When I came into the bedroom minutes ago, she was already asleep. I didn't bother with closing the bathroom door in case she woke up and needed me. That and my only focus had been on taking care of the hard-on I had been sporting since I had my hands on her naked body. Fuck, Vayda's body is like a work of art. Her skin is like silk, and she has curves in all the right places. Had Vayda not been in her current state, my cock would have been balls deep inside what I know will be the sweetest fucking pussy I'd ever taste. But I behaved and kept my dick under wraps. I wasn't the only one affected by the moment either. Oh, Vayda was aching for my touch...my cock. I could taste it in the air. I smelled her arousal, and my mouth watered at the thought of getting a taste, of sliding my tongue through her slit and lapping up every drop of honey she had to offer. The lips of Vayda's pussy were dripping, and it wasn't the water from her bath.

Closing my eyes, my nostrils flare as I suck in her faint scent that still lingers in the air, and I work my palm up and down my cock. I turn my body slightly to give Vayda a show. I let her see how much she affects me; how hard my cock is for her. What I'm doing is so fucking wrong on more levels than I can count, yet I am powerless to stop it. When this thing between Vayda and I is said and done, she is going to hate me. When she discovers the truth, unlocking a world of hurt and betrayal, I'm going to hate myself. And since I'm most likely going to hell for my many sins, I may as well have a little taste of heaven on earth while I can. I'm going to give in to my desires and fall headfirst into the abyss. Because the force that woman has on me leaves no other choice. It's just too bad it's not Vayda's pussy squeezing the hell out of my dick right now. On that thought, I open my eyes, turn my head, and stare out the glass door of the shower.

The steam of the hot water and the darkness of the bedroom make it impossible for me to make eye contact with the woman who I know is watching me work my cock. I can feel her heated gaze searing straight through me. Vayda's gaze is what has a familiar tingle shooting up the base of my spine as my balls draw up. My jaw tenses as my fist continues to tug on my cock, drawing my orgasm from my body. I growl out Vayda's name the moment my release barrels through me. I refuse to break the invisible, yet tangible connection Vayda and I are currently locked in. Not until I have stroked every last drop of cum from my cock, and it washes down the drain.

Once I have finished with my shower and given my cock some much-needed relief, I dress in a pair of black boxer briefs. Flicking the light off, I step out of the bathroom and into the bedroom.

As expected, Vayda lies awake in bed, utterly unembarrassed about being caught watching me jack off in the shower. That's Vayda for you though. She's not one to shy away and get embarrassed easily. She also has never hidden her attraction for me. Unmoving, I stay rooted in place while the two of us engage in some silent stare-off. Something we seem to do a lot of lately.

Both are waiting to see what the other will say or do first.

Vayda's looks are one of a challenge—always have been. My stares are usually one I try to mask with indifference. My mask is a lie except for tonight. Tonight, there is only truth in my gaze. My truth...want. I want this beautiful creature lying in front of me so bad my fingers twitch at my sides with the thought of touching her. I came in the shower, not ten minutes ago, and already my dick is standing at attention. Vayda notices too because she breaks eye contact long enough for her eyes to travel south. Her breath hitches. Not only does her breathing change right before me, but the blanket covering her body rustles as she starts rubbing her thighs together. Vayda aches for me, her pussy desperate for relief.

Tossing all boundaries between us out the window, I cross the distance between us in three long strides where I come to stand beside the bed. Vayda's breathing intensifies with my being so close. Without a second thought, I drop to one knee while tossing the blanket to the side in one fell swoop to find Vayda wearing nothing. "I would ask if you liked what you saw, but I can smell your pussy from here, and your pussy says you did." I rest my heavy palm at the top of Vayda's stomach, my fingers barely caressing her soft skin. A tiny moan escapes her lips as her eyes glaze over with lust. "Does that sweet pussy ache, baby?"

"Yes," Vayda rasps. "Make it go away."

"I'll make you feel better, baby." I bring my mouth next to her ear where I can't help but inhale her intoxicating scent. "You have to be still for me, though. I don't want you hurting yourself. Can you do that for me? Can you lay still while I take care of this pussy; make it feel better?"

"God, yes, Malik. I'll do anything so long as you touch me. I need you to touch me." Vayda's words drip with desperation.

Rearing back, a mere inch, I keep my face directly in front of hers. My eyes stay locked on Vayda's while my hand slides further south until the tips of my fingers brush over her throbbing, wet clit. Vayda sucks in a sharp breath.

"Malik."

"So fuckin' wet for me." My finger slips through her slit, gathering her wetness before sinking into her tight hole. Curving upward, I find her sweet spot the same time my palm presses down on her clit. Adding a second finger, I start to thrust in and out while making sure to pay special attention to both places that have her on the verge of combustion. "The next time I make you come, it's going to be with my mouth. I can't wait to have you sit on my face so I can fuck you with my tongue and take everything your greedy pussy wants to give me." My promise causes Vayda's eyes to flair. "You want that, don't you, baby? You want to climb on my face and let me eat that pussy until I get my fill."

Overcome with pleasure and unable to speak, Vayda nods. I know she is close and on the verge of coming when her heat floods my palm and her walls begin to flutter around my fingers. She was already on edge, so it doesn't take long for her orgasm to build. Her pussy hasn't come yet, and it's squeezing the hell out of my finger. I can't imagine what it will feel like when I get my cock in there.

When Vayda starts to chase her release by wiggling her hips, my movements pause.

"No, Malik! Don't stop. I was close."

"I told you not to move."

Vayda glares. "I won't. Just don't stop."

Giving her what she needs, I continue my ministries. When I enter her pussy a second time and zero in on her g-spot, her walls clamp down around my fingers. Snaking my free hand under Vayda's head, I lean down and cover her mouth with my own, swallowing her orgasm. I wait for the last spasm to wreck her body before reluctantly releasing her lips and slipping my hand from between us. Leaning back, I take in the sated, dreamy look on Vayda's face. I have a feeling it will become one of my favorite looks on her; one I'll make sure she wears often. A woman like

Vayda deserves all the pleasures of the world. And with her heat still coating my hand, I do something I have been dying to do for longer than I care to admit. I bring my fingers to my mouth and take the first taste of my woman. Vayda's golden irises track my movement as I do. "You taste just like I knew you would." "And what's that?" she asks, her voice raspy.

"Like heaven on earth."

---

The next morning, I arrive at the clubhouse around 10:00 am.

After I made breakfast for Vayda, she surprised me by asking if Josie would be back over to visit her today. I wasn't surprised to find the two have become friends. Knowing Josie, she had a conversation with Vayda putting her mind at ease about things between us.

"Hey, brother. You ready to get on the road?" Riggs asks when I climb off my bike. The club is heading to Lake Charles today for a charity event. Clubs from the surrounding states will meet up with us to raise money for our veterans—a cause Riggs and I are passionate about and take part in every year for the last four years. There will be live music, food trucks, raffles, and all sorts of fun and games for the kids. The event is family friendly and pulls in hundreds of spectators. Last year we raised nearly seventy thousand dollars. Our goal this year is one hundred thousand. Although I suspect the turnout will be much larger considering we got a call last month from Quinn, a member of our Montana chapter, saying his wife arranged for her brother's band to play at this year's event. East of Addiction is known all over the world, and we lucked out, getting them to donate their time. It pays to have connections.

"Yeah, Prez. I'm good to go."

Riggs strides up to me with Luna at his side. She will be

making the three-hour trip with us along with Piper, who will be riding with her dad.

"I talked to Chief Richards this morning. He said he would have one of his men stationed outside your place while we are gone. Just to be on the safe side. Also, Josie is on her way over there now to hang with your girl."

This is why I'd do anything for the man standing in front of me. "Thanks, Prez. I appreciate ya looking out for her."

"We take care of our own."

Halfway to Lake Charles, we meet up with Knight Warriors MC from Rockwood, Tennessee. Grizz and his men, Smokey, Skinner, and Gunner were stopped at a gas station where we had made a pit stop. Their club has participated in the same charity event each year it's been held. Although this is the first time I've seen a woman on the back of their president's bike. Grizz introduced Noel as his Old Lady. Grizz and his men are reliable, and the two clubs get along well.

We arrive at the location of the event to see Easton and his band already here and ready to set up. The other guys and I pull up and park right next to their tour bus, our engines alerting them to our arrival. Easton steps out of the bus and strides up to Riggs, offering him a hand. He does the same with me.

"We're glad you could make it, man," I tell him.

"The guys and I are happy to help any way we can. It's the least we can do."

A couple of hours later the music is jumping with East of Addiction killing it up on stage. The weather has cooperated even though there was a threat of rain, and we have had triple attendance turnout. The guys and I are sitting under a tent tossing back a cold beer and eating some of Louisiana's finest gumbo when I catch sight of something out of the corner of my eye. I do a double take. When I realize my eyes are not deceiving me, every sense in my body goes on high alert. The hairs on the back of my neck stand on end. Riggs, who is seated beside me with Luna on his lap, must sense something because his demeanor changes when he takes note of my body language. His eyes travel in the direction of mine. "You see what I'm seein', Prez?"

"What the fuck?" Those words coming from Riggs' mouth draws the attention of Fender, Kiwi, and Everest, who are seated with us.

"What the fuck are Los Demonios doing in the States?" I growl. "Has Jake mentioned anything about them lately?"

"Nope. I'm guessin' he doesn't know they are back. If he did, he would have said somethin'," Riggs assures.

Prez is right. No way Jake would know those fuckers have turned back up and not given us a heads up. A few years ago, Jake and his club had a run-in with Los Demonios. They kidnapped his VP's Old Lady and wreaked a whole fuck ton of havoc on The Kings. The Demonios that had taken up residence in Montana had been wiped out. The club is based out of Mexico and, for the most part, stays on their side of the border. "Them being here is not sittin' right with me, Prez."

No sooner do the words leave my mouth, a commotion can be heard from several yards behind us. I turn my head in that direction to see a fight has broken out. My blood runs cold at what I see before me. Nova has a Los Demonios pinned to the ground with his gun pressed against his head and Piper standing behind him in tears. I waste no time flying from my seat, drawing my piece, and rushing toward the scene.

Behind me, Riggs thrusts Luna into Everest's arms and orders him to get her out of here. Everest does as he's told while Kiwi and Fender trail behind me. "Kiwi, get Piper!" I order. Kiwi immediately scoops Piper up. Piper tries to struggle against his hold, worried about her dad. When another Demonios steps in front of him to block his path, he clocks the son of a bitch in the jaw, knocking him to the ground. Not once does Kiwi lose his hold on Piper. I briefly notice Grizz entering the picture as he sends two of his men with Kiwi.

As I make it to where Nova still has a man pinned to the ground, I intervene on an asshole who was about to sucker punch my brother from behind. "Only pussies strike when their opponent isn't lookin'," I spit just before my fist makes contact with his nose. Seconds later the event has turned into pure chaos as parents grab their children and run. To my left I see Fender punch another Demonios the same time Riggs fends off another. With the guy I just sent for a nap forgotten, I turn my attention back to Nova. I don't make it two steps when another asshole comes up behind me. I feel his approach before I see it. Twisting, I bring my right arm up and block the hand with a knife currently in its grasp, land a punch to the guy's gut the same moment I twist his wrist until I feel his bone snap. The man bellows in pain as the knife falls to the ground. I kick the blade out of reach then finish him off with a blow to the jaw. He falls in a heap next to his buddy on the ground. It's also then I see a man break through the crowd, draw his gun and set his sight on Nova.

Stepping in front of my brother, I aim my pistol at the Demonios. "Not today, motherfucker."

The Demonios refuse to relent. "Call your man off."

It is Nova who speaks next. "This son of a bitch put his hands on my daughter."

That one statement has my blood running cold. From the corner of my eye, I notice Nova's words have had the same effect on Riggs and Fender. The man in Nova's grasp has sealed his fate. There is no way he is letting that man walk away alive. The sound of police sirens blare in the distance. I look around to see there is not one spectator in sight. Grizz and his men are standing off to the side ready to have our backs. Their assistance is not needed though. Los Demonios are sorely outnumbered. The man who currently has his gun on Nova is the only one left standing. Riggs is the next to speak, his words directed at Nova.

"Cane. The cops are coming in hot. We need to ride out, brother." Riggs gestures to the soon to be dead man. "You know you can't do that here."

"Yeah, puta," the guy Nova has pinned spits. "Listen to your friend and let me go." The man smirks. Both sides know we can't do shit out in the open like this.

The Demonios standing in front of me with his weapon still aimed at Nova says something to his men in Spanish. Knowing there is no other option with the police sirens getting closer, he slowly steps back while his guys who have picked themselves up off the ground follow suit. With all the strength he can muster, Nova releases the bastard underneath him, but not before he delivers a promise. "I'll be seeing you real soon."

At Nova's threat, I look to Fender and give him the signal. He nods and discreetly steps away from us and heads in the direction of his bike. I cut my eyes to Riggs, who nods in approval. I sent Fender on a mission to follow those low life pussies. Because my brother is going to make good on his promise, we'll be seeing these fuckers soon.

Nobody says a word to Nova as we hightail it to our bikes. When we approach Easton's tour bus where Grizz's guys are standing guard, Kiwi and Easton step off with Luna and Piper,

who runs into her dad's arms. "Dad!"

Nova scoops his daughter up. "I'm okay, Bean."

"I was so scared something was going to happen to you."

"I wouldn't let anything happen, sweetheart."

While Nova and Piper have their moment, Riggs cuts in. "We need to haul ass now." Riggs addresses Easton. "You stayin' close by?"

"The guys and I are staying at a hotel about five miles up the road. Why?"

"We're going to follow you there. I'm gonna need someone to stay with Luna and Piper while my guys and I handle somethin'."

"You got it," Easton nods, turns on his heel, and jumps back on the bus. The rest of us climb on our bikes and peel out of the parking lot. The club will face some fallout for what happened here today, but we have a few connections to help smooth shit over and assure there will be no repercussions. We can't risk the future of this event.

Minutes later we make it to the hotel. Riggs orders Everest to stay with Luna and Piper on Easton's bus. Luckily after the initial shock of what went down has worn off, Piper is in full-on fan-girl mode. Easton has turned out to be the perfect distraction, which is a good thing because while we wait on word from Fender, Nova is on the verge of losing his shit. Sitting on my bike, I take a drag off my cigarette while watching my brother pace in front of me. There is no calming Nova down when he gets like this. His daughter is his world, and the man who put his hands on her will not be escaping the grim reaper tonight.

Fifty minutes later, Riggs gets the call we've been waiting for. He places the phone to his ear, listens for a moment then hangs up. "Fender has eyes on them. Let's ride."

No other words are spoken, no questions asked. I, along with Nova and Kiwi, fall in behind our Prez as we seek retribution. And retribution we will have.

It turns out Los Demonios are camped out by the river one town over. The sun has set by the time we reach them. Fender is waiting on us half a mile up the road from where they are. "How many we got?" I ask, dismounting my bike.

"There are five of them. Fuckers look like they've been hangin' around a few days. They got tents and shit set up down by the river."

"How do you want to approach, Prez?" I ask.

"We go on foot from here. Kiwi, you and Fender circle round

and come up behind them on the east side of the river. Nova, Wick, and I will assess our surroundings from the west. Wait for my move. You all know what to do. Also, there were six of their men at the event. Be on the lookout for the sixth asshole."

We reach the site where Los Demonios are currently held up. They have a small fire going, and all five men are in sight. All five men look to be drinking heavily, as well and making our task more manageable. The fuckers don't have enough sense to watch their backs after the stunt they pulled. I guess they figured The Kings would go on our merry way. They will learn the hard way how wrong they are.

"I don't know about you, Prez, but I say we go in. I'm ready to get back home."

"I'm with you, brother. Let's end this shit and go home."

Nova's murderous energy vibrates off him as he steps up beside me. "The one who touched my daughter is mine."

With those final words, Nova, Riggs, and I sprint out of the woods. Our takedown happens in the blink of an eye. We charge the campsite with our weapons drawn. Gunfire erupts, sending men to the ground simultaneously ducking for cover. I take protection just as a bullet rips the bark off the tree that shields me. I wait a beat before I step out from behind the tree. My eyes zero in on a guy hunkered down behind a motorcycle. With the top of his head visible, I take my shot. The second the guy's body slumps over, I seek out my next target.

"Clear!" Riggs calls out.

Holstering my weapon, I take in the makeshift campsite to see four of the five Demonios dead. All except the one Nova has pinned up against a tree a few yards away. Us men make our way toward him and stand at his back while he delivers his justice. The guy struggles against Nova's hold, but the look in his eyes says he knows his time on earth has come to an end. With his blade resting against the neck of the man who made the grave mistake of putting his hands on Piper, Nova delivers his last words. "I told you I'd be seein' you." The blade of his knife slides across the man's neck, and we all watch as life drains from the guy's soulless eyes as he's sent straight to hell, where he will be greeted by the devil himself. There are no second chances for men who dare to touch one of our own.

We make it back to the hotel thirty minutes later, not bothering to dispose of the evidence we left behind. The gators will do that for us. Easton asks only one question when we find him standing outside the hotel smoking a cigarette while Nova and Riggs go collect the girls. "You get your shit squared away?"

I stay rooted on my bike as I take a drag from my cigarette and regard the rockstar boy in front of me for a long moment. "Yep."

Easton tosses his butt to the ground. "Hit me up again next year. You guys know how to throw one hell of a party."

The ride back to New Orleans is spent with me replaying today's events in my head. Riggs assured him he was going to contact Jake to see if he had any intel on why Los Demonios have crossed the border. I can't help but think there is something shady about their timing. Why now? Why Louisiana? There is also the question of the other man who was at the event but not the campsite. He'll be in for one hell of a surprise when he returns to his buddies to find them dead. That's if the swamps of Louisiana haven't gotten to them first.

It's nearly 2:00 am when we ride back into New Orleans. Riggs and the rest of the guys head on to the clubhouse while I take the exit that takes me to my house. As soon as I turn on my street, I breathe a sigh of relief, and a fraction of the tension weighing me down evaporates when I see the police cruiser sitting outside my home. Pulling up to the squad car, I idle next to the driver's side window. "Wick," the officer greets.

"Any issues tonight?" I ask.

"Nope. All is quiet. One of your girls left here around ten. She came out to my car to report she set the alarm, and your guest was getting ready to turn in for the night."

"Thanks for watching the place, Kent." I stick my palm out and shake the officer's hand. Kent Brower has been on the force as long as I've lived in New Orleans. He's a solid guy and is always ready to lend a helping hand to the club.

As Kent takes off down the street, I steer my bike into the garage. It's been a long fucking day, and the only thing I want is to put eyes on my girl.

# 12

# TEQUILA

Last night and again this morning, I chose to stay quiet and have patience. Neither Malik nor I discussed what took place after his shower. Once we both came down from the high we were riding, Malik crawled into the bed behind me, pulled the blanket over the two of us, and we fell asleep. To be honest, I don't think either one of us was ready to talk about it— about us. The moment would not have been what it was if we had further complicated what is already looming between the two of us. I think we both needed the simplicity and peace right after what we did. And it's been a long time coming. Malik has avoided the fire between us for years, never letting himself get closer than he was.

I felt him when he left the bed this morning, taking his soothing body heat with him. As quiet as he was, I figured he didn't want to disturb me, or maybe he wanted to avoid the inevitable. Nevertheless, I bit my tongue and kept my eyes closed, pretending to still be asleep as he pressed his lips to my temple, not once, but twice, then walked out of the bedroom. Only when I heard the rumble of his Harley did I open my eyes. I laid there for more than thirty minutes before getting my sore body out of bed.

I've had all day to think about everything. Me, Malik, us. Nothing more to do than to get lost in my own head while wandering around this baren house. Most of my day was spent upstairs until I received a text from a phone number I didn't recognize but turned out to be Josie's. I'm not mad; after the chat she and I had yesterday, we know enough about one another that I can safely say I'm okay with her. She texted that she would be making a grocery run and wanted to see if I needed anything specific. It turns out I did. Forty minutes later, she showed up to the house with a trunk full of groceries, which I tried to help her unload, but she wasn't having it. Neither were my ribs. A fucking eight-pound bag felt like trying to carry a large child thanks to my broken bones.

Josie didn't stay long, mainly because my body kept screaming at me to get more rest so it could heal. Instead of what I would typically do, which would be to push my body harder, to make myself push through any discomfort or pain, I listened to it, and carried my ass back up the stairs with a plate of my favorite snacks: strawberries, cheese cubes, Honeycrisp apple slices, and a whole jar of feta cheese stuffed green olives. Josie laughed at my food choices, claiming only a pregnant woman would eat a combination like that. She spun around, with a serious look on her face and asked me if I was pregnant. I damn near choked on the olive I had just popped in my mouth when the question passed her lips, then informed her I hadn't had a decent dicking in months, so there is no way in hell I am pregnant. For a minute, I found myself wanting to talk with Josie about Malik; to get another woman's perspective on things.

For the better part of my life, I've found myself to be more comfortable around men. Not that I haven't had female friends. It's just that ever since serving my country, I find myself working with men more than women, and, in turn, some close friendships have formed with a few of those men I have worked with over the years. It would be nice to have someone without a dick between their legs to talk to. In the end, I decided to keep things to myself.

I'm standing in the kitchen when Malik arrives. Hearing him pull his bike into the garage, I grab a couple of paper plates from the package sitting on the counter beside me.

"It smells good in here." Malik walks into the kitchen. He tosses his keys on top of the island, then shrugs off his cut, and places it on the counter as well.

"I had planned on cooking something for dinner but overslept. I hope you don't mind Chinese takeout." Grabbing the container, I scoop both of us a generous serving of General Tso's chicken with rice onto the plates.

"It's late. You didn't have to wait for me."

Sliding his paper plate toward him, I hand Malik a plastic fork. "I don't mind. Can't sleep." My eyes lift to his. "I have a lot on my mind."

Malik studies me for a moment while taking a bite of his meal. He sighs. "Me too."

The air in the room becomes thick. "Listen—"

"Vayda, I'm sorry." The apology leaves his mouth before I can finish what I was about to say. He puts his fork down and pushes his plate to the side. "This thing between us. The shit that has been brewing for too many damn years." Malik steps to my side, invading my space and my senses. "I'm tired of fighting it. I'm fucking exhausted from fighting it."

My insides feel like combusting with his admission, but I can still see the struggle behind his domineering brown eyes. Something is holding him back from completely giving in to what I know we both want, and I cup his cheek in the palm of my hand. Malik leans into it, seeking the comfort of my touch, and that alone causes my heart to smile. "But?" I inquire knowing something deeper is bothering him, that there must be a root to the reason he struggles.

"I want us, baby. I want you. There is no doubt in my mind, in my heart, when it comes to you." His eyes close. "But my head is all fucked up, Vayda. You're my best friend's sister."

"Somehow, I don't think my brother would have had an issue with us being together, Malik. He loved me." I brush his cheek with the pad of my thumb. "And he loved you too." My words literally cause Malik to flinch beneath my touch. He takes a step back, and my hand drops to my side.

"You wouldn't say that if you knew." His voice becomes filled with sadness.

"What the hell are you talking about?" I take a step toward him, and he takes another step back. The gesture guts my insides. Frustration overtakes me. I become angry. Angry for the way he has avoided me all these years. Hurt towards the way he is shutting down again when I thought we were moving past all this bullshit. In turn, I bite back. "What is it, huh? Talk to me, Malik," I plead. "What is keeping you from giving in to this?" I point to him and myself. "You just told me you wanted me, but just as fast you back away as if my touch repulses you?"

Without warning, Malik rages, screaming at the top of his lungs. "It's my fault, Vayda. It's my fault Damien is dead!"

Momentarily stunned by his outburst, I stand rooted in place. Turning around, Malik puts his fist through the wall. "It shouldn't have happened. He should have let me die that day. He should have lived." His shoulders rise and fall with his rapid breathing.

Approaching him, I wrap my arms around him from behind, placing my hands on his chest and resting my cheek against his back. I realize, as I listen to his heart pound hard against my ear and feel it beating against my palms, we've never actually talked about the day my brother died. "It wasn't your fault."

Malik takes in a shuddered breath, but remains facing the wall, with his hands braced against it and hangs his head. "You weren't there. If only—." He doesn't finish his sentence.

"I've seen the report. Daddy got his hands on the statement you and the other soldiers in your unit gave as well, Malik. If he would have been wearing his headgear, then yes, he most likely would have made it through the incident on that particular day. But there is no guarantee he would still be here today. That's the risk he was willing to take. He knew there was a chance he would never come home. It's a choice we all make every day." Malik stays silent, so I keep going. "He died trying to save you. He was doing what any best friend—a brother would do. He made a choice that day, Malik."

"And I live with his choice every day, and those scars are more profound than the visible ones I wear on my body."

Ducking under his arm, I insert myself between him and the wall, and it forces him to look at me. Tears well in my eyes when I notice the hurt in his as he stares deep into my soul. "I can't get the image out of my head, baby. I close my eyes, and he is all I see. That day haunts me, and as much as I know I should move on, I can't," Malik admits. His gaze drops to my lips. "You want to know what's fucked up? I'm baring my soul to you, letting you in to see the demons I battle against on a daily basis, and the hardest battle of them all is trying not to kiss you right now."

I feel lightheaded. Malik has this effect on me, and right now, I want nothing more than for what I'm feeling to consume me. My eyes fall to his lips. "I want you to kiss me too." Malik doesn't give me time to breathe before his mouth captures mine. He kisses me as I have never been kissed before, and I lose myself in it. It feels like the floor beneath us disappears. My entire body becomes weightless as we consume each other. The kiss is messy and desperate. It's perfect. All the air leaves my body once he breaks our connection.

Malik rests his forehead to mine, both of us panting. "I want this. I want us."

"Are you sure?" I ask him, hoping he says yes.

"Fuckin' positive. Right now, it's the only thing I know I'm sure of." With ease, Malik scoops me into his arms. Without asking why, I wrap my arms around his neck as he carries me out of the kitchen, leaving our forgotten food on the counter and brings me up the stairs. He sets me on my feet. I can't take my eyes off him as he begins to strip his clothes from his body. Desire takes over, but so does apprehension. Hesitant because anything more physical than walking would surely hurt like hell. Malik reads me like an open book. Leaving his boxers on, he steps up to me, the thin tank I'm wearing does nothing to hide my body's reaction to him, and my nipples protrude against the fabric. His palm slides from my shoulder down my arm, and he kisses my forehead. "Not tonight, baby." My shoulders sag. "Don't get it twisted. I want to fuck you." He lifts my chin. "I'm going to fuck you. But not until you have healed enough to do so. Got it?" He waits for my reply, and I nod. "Words, Vayda."

"Got it."

His brow raises, and the corner of his lip turns up. "Got what?"

I hold his stare, with a grin of my own. "You will fuck me."

After settling me into the bed, Malik walks to the other side, switches the lamp off, and slides in behind me. Resting his palm on my hip, he buries his face in the crook of my neck. "For now, holding you is just as good." I smile. "Vayda?"

"Yeah?"

"I've been fighting it for so long, thinking I was doing the right thing, but I was lying to myself." He pauses, then finishes. "It's always been you. Since the night I took you to homecoming, I knew."

"Knew what?" I hold my breath.

"You are mine. You have always been mine."

The following morning, I wake to my phone ringing and Malik's palm gripping my upper thigh, his pinky finger dangerously close to my lady bits. Then his hand flexes. "You going to answer that?"

Sighing, I slowly grab my phone from the nightstand and notice my dad's face lighting up the screen. "Hey, Daddy," I answer in a sleepy tone.

"Hey, Pumpkin. You got a minute?" The tone in his voice concerns me. Carefully easing myself into an upright position, I lean my back against the headboard.

"Daddy, is everything okay?" My words cause Malik to sit up in bed as well. His face shows concern as I look at him with worry of my own.

"Uh, well." My dad draws out his words, and I picture him rubbing the back of his head. "You won't believe who is sitting in my living room on my couch at the moment."

I scrunch my forehead. "Who?"

"Georgia."

"Georgia?" I look at Malik and wait for the name to resonate with him, which only takes a second. "What is she doing there? Hell, what is she doing back in Texas?" I ask. Come to think of it; I haven't seen her since Damien died. Two months after his service, she left and moved to another state. The last time I spoke to her, she said she couldn't breathe in our hometown anymore. That the memory of my brother was etched on every surface around her, and it was suffocating her. "Daddy, are you still there?" I ask as silence looms between us.

"She's been here since Monday. She needs help, Pumpkin. She's in bad shape."

"Okay, so what does that have to do with us?" I huff.

"She's asking us to take her daughter."

"Daddy," I sigh. He has a big heart and is always trying to help others, but he's biting off more than he can chew with this case. "I think-."

"Vayda, she says the kid is Damien's."

It takes my brain a minute to catch up to what he said. Then I process his words a couple of times before responding. I roll my eyes. "Daddy, really? How old is this kid?" I start to get angry that she's taking advantage of his kind heart.

"Her name is Sydney, and she's eleven years old."

I do the math in my head, and if I were standing, Malik would be picking my ass up off the floor.

"Pumpkin. Come home." Something in the tone of his voice kicks my ass into gear.

"I'll see you in a few hours," I tell him.

He lets out a sigh of relief. "Thank you."

Before disconnecting the call, I tell him, "I love you, Daddy."

"I love you too, Pumpkin."

Placing my phone back on the nightstand, still in disbelief, I face Malik, and stare blankly at him. "Well?" he waits.

"Georgia showed up on my dad's doorstep, with a kid, claiming she is Damien's," I rush my words.

"Wait. Back up a bit. Georgia showed up after almost twelve years saying her kid is Damien's?"

"Yes," I confirm what I just said.

"Okay. Well, that's what DNA tests are for." He scrubs his palm down his face, trying to grasp the information. "Baby, you know there's a possibility she's telling the truth. He was eager to get back home because if memory serves me, she kept telling him she had a surprise for him."

I shake my head. "Why wait eleven years?"

"I don't know, babe. We don't know her story. That's something only she can answer."

"Malik. Daddy said she was in bad shape, and she wants my family to take her daughter." Getting out of bed, I cross the room and begin to peel my sleep clothes off, replacing them with black ripped jeans, and a loose shirt. Following my lead, Malik rises from the bed and throws some clothes on as well.

"He didn't say what he meant by bad shape?" Malik sits on the side of the bed and ties his boot laces. Standing, he strides across the room and plucks my boots off the floor. "Sit." He points to the bed, and I do as he says. Slipping my feet into my shoes, Malik squats and laces them for me. "We'll grab some coffee and something to eat before leaving town."

Even though I managed to walk up and down the stairs on my own for the past two days, Malik insists on helping me, holding me around my waist. "You don't have to hold me. I have the railing to hold onto." I roll my eyes.

"Zip it. I'm helping you, so get over it." His lip twitches when I narrow my eyes at him, but again, I keep my mouth shut.

Once downstairs, he quickly grabs his keys and cut from the counter. "Wait, I should clean the kitchen. We left food out last night." I try telling him as he ushers me to the door leading to the garage.

"Leave it. I'll get one of the girls to come by and take care of it." We enter the garage. Parked beside his bike is a brand new four door black truck.

"Why so big?" I raise my brow. "You know what they say about men and big trucks?" I say to get a rise out of him.

Stopping, he spins, facing me, and presses his hard body against mine. "That's a lie, and you know it." Grabbing my ass, he thrusts into me further. I feel the heat rise on my neck and cheeks as an ache grows between my thighs. "Your sassy mouth makes my blood boil sometimes, but it also makes my dick hard as nails." His head dips, and he gives me a brief kiss, slightly sucking my bottom lip into his mouth. Our lips part. "I plan on fuckin' you senseless, Vayda." Stepping back, he opens the truck door and helps me in, leaving me at a loss for words as he closes the door.

I can see now; this man will use the power of the 'D' against me. And if his kiss or even his magical fingers are any indications to what lies ahead, I am done for.

With coffee and sausage biscuits sitting between us, we hit the interstate, heading west toward the Louisiana-Texas state line. Pressing a button on the steering wheel, a telephone ringing comes through the truck speakers, followed by Riggs' voice filling the cabin. "How's it goin', brother?"

I sip on my coffee as Malik talks. "Sorry to bother you, Prez. I'm callin' to let you know I won't be in town for a day or two."

I hear Riggs whisper something but can't make out the words before he replies. "Everything okay?"

"Yeah. Vayda's dad called this morning, and she needs to get home to deal with a few things."

"Alright. I'll get my brother to fill in for you at the bar until you get back. Where are you now?" Riggs asks.

"On the road. I'll touch base with you later."

"Stay safe," Riggs tells him before the line goes dead.

"Thanks for not saying more until we know for certain what is going on." Picking up my fast food biscuit, I unwrap it to take a bite, but can't seem to stomach eating anything due to the stress I'm feeling, so I place it back into the paper bag. Malik reaches across the console, grabs my hand, pulls it to his mouth, and kisses the back of my knuckles. He doesn't say anything. Our arms rest between us as we hold each other's hands. And it is precisely what I needed.

A few hours later, we pull into my dad's driveway. I haven't been this nervous in a long time, but I find my stomach in knots the moment Malik cuts the engine off. We exit the truck, and Malik is by my side, grabbing my hand in his as we walk toward the front door. "It will be okay. Just think, you could walk away from all of this with a niece."

Sucking in a breath, I reach for the handle on the front door just as it swings open, and we are greeted by my Dad. "Hey, Daddy." He looks from me to Malik, a bit surprised to see him standing beside me, then his eyes drop to our joined hands, and he smiles.

"Hey, Pumpkin." He kisses my cheek then turns to Malik. "Son, it's good to see you." Using his other hand, so he doesn't have to let loose of mine, Malik shakes my dad's hand.

"Good to see you, Sir."

"Come in." My dad steps to the side, and we walk in. My dad looks at me, and his face softens. I take in how tired he looks, and the fact that his eyes are red-rimmed like he may have been crying.

"You okay, Daddy?" I worry.

"It's been a long day so far, Pumpkin, but I'm okay. Now, what do you say we meet Sydney?" He says her name as if he's known her all her life, and I watch his eyes become misty.

Malik and I follow my dad into the living room. The moment we round the corner my eyes fall on a thin tan-skinned girl with long curly hair. Stopping dead in my tracks, I take her in. She's dressed in ripped jeans, a tank top, combat boots, and a flannel shirt tied around her waist. In her blue eyes, I see her mom, Georgia, but everything else about her looks like the female version of my brother.

"Jesus. She looks like the female equivalent of Damien," Malik murmurs. "She looks like you," Malik says as I continue to stare.

"Sydney, this is my daughter, Vayda," my dad introduces us.

Sydney eyes me. Her judgmental gaze looks at me before taking in the big man standing beside me but says nothing. Her mom, my brother's ex, rises from the couch beside her. I was so focused on Sydney; I didn't see her sitting there. I almost don't recognize the woman crossing the room in my direction. Georgia is a former shell of who she once was. The person I once knew was radiant. Beautiful blonde hair that is now thin and dull, sparkling blue eyes that are now sad, almost lifeless. It's her weight that stands out the most. She is tiny. Too thin. "Vayda, it's good to see you."

I force a smile. "It's been a long time." Finding it hard to keep my eyes off her daughter, I look past her.

"Malik?" She directs her attention to my man.

"Georgia." Malik looks down at her, his arms folded across his broad chest.

She smiles at him. "I always knew you two would end up together. It was written in the stars." Georgia turns her head, looking at her daughter, who sits on the couch, looking down at her phone. "Nothing I say will ever be a good enough excuse. I kept her from her family. I was wrong, and for that, I am sorry."

"Why now?" My tone is laced with anger.

"I'm sick, and I need help. But I can't do it on my own." I look at her. I mean, really look at her. "I never meant for it to get out of control."

"Drugs?" Malik says it for me. Georgia just hangs her head.

"Were you using while pregnant?" The thought of anyone being so selfish makes me angrier.

Her head shakes vigorously. "No—never." Georgia looks at her daughter again. "Loving your brother and having Sydney are the two things I know I've done right in my life. My depression got worse after giving birth to mine and Damien's daughter. I couldn't seem to dig my way out of the hole I found myself in. The doctors called it postpartum depression. I just thought it was because I was lost, and my heart was broken. I thought having Sydney around would fix everything—fix me. It felt like nothing they put me on was working. I managed to get through my days. I've taken care of her the best I can. For eleven years, I've been surviving just to make it to the next day." Georgia begins to cry, and her daughter is instantly at her side.

"Mom. You should rest. Let's go home." Sydney almost begs her mother, as her eyes dart between me, Malik, and my dad.

"No. I'm fine. Go sit down, please," Georgia assures her daughter and waits for her to follow orders before she continues. "We'd be here for several more days if I gave you an in-depth look at my life since losing Damien." Georgia looks at me. "Your brother was my everything, and I'm letting him down. I'm letting our daughter down and merely surviving. I need help. I need to learn to live. I need to get better not just for my daughter but for myself, which is why I am here. I need to go away for a while."

Malik inserts himself, asking a fundamental question. "Not to sound like a dick here, but we don't know any of this to be true. You can't just claim for your child to be Damien's daughter without proof."

Georgia's eyes cut to my dad. "Mr. Wilder offered up a DNA sample two days ago." I'm taken back by her statement. My dad never mentioned this to me over the phone.

"The results should be in before the end of the day. A friend of mine has taken care of everything herself and will call as soon as she has news." My dad informs us, and I become pissed because I'm the last to know this little bit of information. "Before you go running your mouth," my dad directs his words at me, "this is my house, and it was my choice. If there is any chance Sydney is my granddaughter I want to know, and I needed to know as quickly as possible. Keep all that in mind before you say another word." He warns me, and I give Malik side-eyes as he suppresses his amusement at my dad scolding me. Mainly because he knows I won't sass my father.

Taking a deep breath, I ask Georgia, "you mentioned going away for a while to get some help. Where?"

"A place in Nevada. It's a rehab facility that specializes in mental health as well as substance abuse. They have a bed available. I've taken out a loan to pay for three months. Unfortunately, insurance doesn't cover this kind of thing." She wrings her hands together. "They can only guarantee my spot for two more days." We can all hear the desperation in her voice.

My dad's phone rings, and we all share a look before he pulls it from his back pocket. "Hello." His eyes stay glued on me as the rest of us continue to hang on by a thin thread. "I'm doing well. Vayda is home," he smiles. "What's the verdict?" The anticipation causes my stomach to knot. "Thank you, hon. We all appreciate it." Finished with his call, he slips the phone back into his pocket and walks away.

"Daddy." I go to follow him, but he turns around, and when he does, his emotions are written on his face. "I have a granddaughter."

Those prove to be the trigger words needed to set off a storm. Sydney flies off the couch, where she had been sitting quietly as her mom had asked. "Mom, please. Don't leave me here. You need me. I need to take care of you." My heart breaks watching her cry. Georgia embraces her.

"Sweetie, I need you too. I need to get better so I can be a better mom for you." She strokes her daughter's hair.

"I'll take care of you," Sydney cries.

"Oh, honey. It's not your job to take care of me. I'm doing what's best for you. I hope one day you will see that." Georgia consoles Sydney.

"I don't know these people. They are not my family." Though she doesn't mean them, Sydney's words hurt me, and I can tell it hurts my dad as well.

Georgia hugs her tight. "That's my fault, Sydney. They are your family, and this is your chance to get to know them."

Needing space to breathe, I head toward the French doors leading to the backyard and step outside. After a couple of minutes, I hear the door open and close behind me just before Malik's strong arms embrace me, pulling my body close to his. He rests his chin on the top of my head. "You have a niece."

"I have a niece." I sound like a parrot repeating his words.

"It's a lot to take in."

I grunt. "You think?" My head falls back against his shoulder. "Does my dad really think he can do this on his own? Take care of an eleven-year-old girl, who will be torn from the only life she has known, to live with a complete stranger?"

The two of us stand in silence, staring out at the yard. "We could take Sydney back home with us." Malik's words have me spinning in his arms and wincing because the sudden movement pulls at my side.

"Are you serious?" I study him, thinking he has lost his mind.

"Why the hell not? You're right. It would be rough on your dad. Besides, we have that huge empty house back home. We have plenty of room." I look at him in wonderment. Malik never ceases to amaze me. His eagerness also scares the shit out of me. I have no idea how to take care of a kid.

"Okay," I tell him without giving any further thought because if I do, I might talk myself out of it. "Let's go tell my dad."

# 13

# WICK

While Vayda, her dad, and Georgia talk alone to hash out their plans on where Sydney will be staying, I decide to go visit my parents while in town. Vayda's father excuses himself from their family gathering and follows me outside. Standing on the front porch, I regard the man in front of me. Mr. Wilder takes a seat on the porch swing and nods toward the chair beside him for me to follow suit.

"First, I want to ask how you're handling all this?"

I sigh and run my palm down my face. "Honestly, I don't think the severity of the situation has hit me yet. I'm on autopilot right now. My main concern is being here for Vayda, giving her the strength and support she needs."

Mr. Wilder nods. "I'd say what you're feeling is completely normal given the circumstances. I didn't want to believe it myself, but one look at the child and..." He lets his statement hang. I think we're all in agreement that the girl inside the house is Damien's even if we didn't have the DNA test to confirm it, which it did.

Both Mr. Wilder and I are silent for a moment before he scoots to the edge of the swing and speaks again. "I want to thank you for taking care of my daughter. Vayda can be stubborn, so I know it was no easy task."

"I'll always take care of her, Sir. I'll protect her and make sure nothing like that happens again," I say with conviction.

"I have no doubt you will, Son. Just remember some things are out of your control and when you find yourself faced with an outcome you aren't expecting, one that leaves you a little lost, just remember it's God's will. He has a plan for us. I think that little girl inside is a true testament to his plan. I know what happened the day my son was killed, Malik. I also know you have been living with pain and guilt. It's time to let it all go. It's time to start living the second chance he gave you instead of merely existing."

"You're right, Mr. Wilder. I'm gettin' there. Vayda has opened my eyes to a lot of things lately. Being around her has made me realize I need to go after the things I want in life and that I deserve to be happy."

"Of course you do, Son. Damien wouldn't have wanted it any other way. If he were here today, he would have kicked your ass for breaking his baby sister's heart."

I snap my head up from looking at my feet.

"Don't look so surprised. I'm old, not dead. My little girl has been in love with you for as long as I can remember and vice versa. If it were any other man, I would have put a bullet in your ass for how you've been acting. I knew you two would find your way eventually." Mr. Wilder stands from the swing, and I do the same. He offers me his hand. "About time you pulled your head out of your ass, Son." We shake hands, and I chuckle as he disappears back inside the house.

A short time later, I'm walking into my parents' home. I call out, "Mom! Dad!"

My mother comes bustling around the corner of the living room with a dish towel in her hands. "Malik!"

"Hey, Mom." I bend down, and she wraps her arms around my neck. "How's my boy doing?" She kisses my cheek.

"I'm good. Is dad around? I wanted to talk to you both."

"Sure. He's out back. I was just about to take his lunch out to him. Are you hungry?"

"I could eat."

"Great. Go on out. I will be there in a minute."

Walking into the kitchen, I step through the screen door and into the backyard to see my dad hunched over on one knee, fiddling with the lawnmower. He looks up from the machine as I step into view. "Malik! You didn't tell us you were coming to town." He tosses the wrench to the ground and stands. I meet him halfway across the yard, and he pulls me in for a hug.

"I hadn't planned on it, but there was sort of an emergency, and I drove Vayda to her dad's place."

"What kind of emergency? Is everything alright?" he asks ushering me to take a seat on a lawn chair by the back door just as my mother comes out with a platter of sandwiches.

"What's going on? Did you say there was an emergency with Vayda? Is it her father?" my mother asks, taking a seat next to my dad.

"Vayda's fine, and so is Mr. Wilder." Both my parents relax.

"Well, what is it, Son?" my dad questions.

"A woman showed up at Mr. Wilder's house the other day. Do you remember that girl Damien was seeing all through high school and up until he died?" My parents nod.

"Georgia showed up with a little girl claiming she was Damien's daughter." My mother gasps and places her hand over her mouth.

"Anyway, the child is eleven years old. The timing of her age and birth match up. Plus, we all know they were together for years. That, and a DNA test proved she's Damien's"

"Why is she just now coming forward? Why keep the child

away from her aunt and grandfather for eleven years?" my father questions.

"Georgia said she doesn't have a good excuse for not telling Damien's family about Sydney, just that she's sorry she did. She came to them because she is going through some personal stuff and needs help with her daughter. She's asking for Vayda's help with Sydney while she straightens her life out. She has no family and doesn't want the state involved. It is obvious she loves her daughter; otherwise she wouldn't have come. Especially knowing how angry Vayda and her dad would be when finding out she has been keeping Damien's daughter a secret."

"What's the plan?" This is coming from my mom.

"Vayda and I are bringing Sydney back to New Orleans with us. We're going to take care of her."

My father lifts a brow. "We?"

I sigh. My dad is giving me a knowing look, and my mother is beaming from ear to ear—both anticipating my response.

"Yes, we. Vayda and Sydney will be staying at my house."

My dad crosses his arms over his broad chest. "Does this mean you finally got your head out of your ass, Son?"

"Why the hell does everyone keep saying that?" I throw myself against the back of the chair and look up at the sky.

"Oh, sweetheart," my mom gushes. "I have been praying for this day to come. I just knew you two were made for each other."

"What?"

My mother rolls her eyes and swats her hand at me. "Oh, please. We all knew this day was coming. I still remember the way you used to look at that girl when you were younger."

Taking pity on me, my dad changes the subject. "Is there anything you need your mom and me to do? You know we'll help anyway we can."

"Thanks, dad. Right now, I'm not sure what we need."

"Have you talked to the guys?"

"Not yet. I was going to do that after talking to you two."

After a quick lunch with my parents, I drive back to Mr. Wilder's house. The vehicle Georgia arrived in is now gone.

Pulling my phone from my pocket, I decide to give Riggs a call.

"Brother."

"Hey, man. The brothers there with ya?"

"Yeah. We're hangin' here at the clubhouse. Let me put you on speaker." There is a pause. "Alright, man. You have our attention."

"I need your help with something."

"You name it."

"You all know Vayda was called home to tend to a family emergency."

"Yeah? Is she good? Her dad, okay?"

"No, no. It's nothing like that. Her dad is fine. The thing is Damien's girlfriend he had before he died showed up out of the blue."

"Okay," Riggs draws. "Where's the problem with that?"

I let out a deep breath. "She showed up with a kid. The little girl, Sydney, is eleven. She's Damien's."

"Jesus fuckin' Christ," Riggs hisses. I can hear the shocked voices of my brothers in the background.

"What's the plan?"

"Vayda and I are bringing Sydney home with us. Think you all can get some shit squared away at my house before we get back?"

Kiwi jumps in on the conversation. "We got you, brother. What do you need?"

I sigh. "Fuck. I need everything—furniture for the living room. I'm going to need someone to stock the fridge and cabinets. I don't have shit to eat in the house, aside from the few things Josie has dropped off since Vayda has been at the house. I don't even know what the kid likes to eat. Maybe I'll have Vayda find out, and I'll text you a list."

"No worries, Wick. I got you covered!" This is coming from Nova.

Piper's ecstatic voice breaks out over the phone. "Oh, my God! Can I decorate her bedroom? Please. It will be so much fun."

I chuckle. "Sure, sweetheart. But nothin' too girly. From the looks of Sydney, she's not into any frilly shit. And no pink."

"No problem. I can work with that. I know exactly what to do," Piper says with excitement.

"Look, brother. You handle your business there, and when you get back, you'll have what you need. We got your back."

"Thanks, Riggs. We'll probably head out first thing in the mornin'."

"Alright, brother. If you need anything else, give me a holler."

After hanging up with Riggs, I sit in the truck for a few minutes to reflect on the random twist of events that have suddenly rained down havoc on mine and Vayda's lives. No matter how out of my element I am or how fucking clueless I am when it comes to raising a kid, I make the silent vow, right here and now, to make Damien proud. I'll look after and protect his daughter just as he would if he were still alive to do it himself.

---

The next morning, we are on the road and heading back to New Orleans. We've been driving for a couple of hours. Sydney has been mostly quiet. When she does speak, it's only to answer a question from myself or Vayda. Her responses are laced with attitude. Vayda is not deterred by Sydney's less than stellar welcoming. Who can blame the kid? She's lashing out because she's hurting. Sydney being standoffish is her way of coping. She's putting up a wall to protect herself. Here she is, an eleven-year-old girl who has been dumped off on strangers by her sick mother. Sydney has no reason to trust Vayda or me and, as a child, she doesn't know any other way to deal with how lost she's feeling at the moment.

Passing the sign for a local diner I eat at every time I drive through Texas, I glance at the time on the dashboard to see it's nearly noon. I turn to Vayda who is sitting in the passenger seat. "How about we stop for lunch and fuel up?"

Vayda nods then turns slightly in the seat to face Sydney, who has been sitting silently in the back seat since we left. "We're going to stop for lunch. You hungry?"

Sydney shrugs her shoulders but remains quiet. Her rebuff does nothing to faze Vayda, though. "Well, I don't know about you, but I'm starving. I could go for a big cheeseburger, fries, and a chocolate shake." Vayda continues to look at Sydney as she talks. The little girl doesn't say anything, but when I look into the rearview mirror, I don't miss the slight smile she quickly tries to hide by turning her head. When Vayda twists back in her seat and looks at me, her smile says she didn't miss it either.

Stopping at the diner turned out to be a good idea. Sydney scarfed down a swiss and bacon cheeseburger, which also happens to be Vayda's favorite, along with fries. She also opted for a strawberry milkshake. I continue to eat my meal as Vayda makes another attempt at small talk.

"So, Sydney. What grade are you in at school?"

Sydney pops a fry in her mouth as she goes about studying Vayda. She surprises us both when she finally answers. "I'm in the sixth grade."

"Do you like school?" Vayda continues.

"Yes. I really like History."

I grin and cut my eyes to Vayda to see her face break out in the biggest smile. "Your dad loved History."

Sydney cracks a smile. "Mom says that too."

Vayda doesn't ask any more questions. She's probably looking at the few sentences she got out of her niece just now as a victory and has decided not to push. Once we have finished our lunch and stopped by the gas station to fuel up, we get back on the road. Before leaving the diner, I sent off a quick text to Riggs letting him know to expect us in a couple more hours.

"She's passed out." Vayda hooks her thumb over her shoulder to Sydney, who has indeed fallen asleep.

"Kid had a long couple of days," I grunt.

"Have you told the guys about her?"

"Talked to Prez yesterday after I visited my parents. The guys are at the house now gettin' it ready."

"Getting it ready?"

"Yeah, baby. I am getting it ready. You know I don't have shit in my house. Told them to buy some furniture, stock the kitchen. Piper was all over the idea of decoratin' Sydney's room."

Vayda looks at me, stunned. "You had them do all that for Sydney?"

"I didn't do it just for Sydney. I did it for you too, Vayda. I want my house to be a home for both of you. I'm all in, Vayda. This thing with Sydney; we're in it together."

Vayda reaches across the armrest and takes hold of my hand. "I don't know what I'd do without you; without the club. You're like home to me, Malik, and the club is like a second family."

Lifting our joined hands to my lips, I kiss the inside of Vayda's wrist.

The sun is just beginning to set by the time I pull into the driveway of my house. Sydney curiously perks up from the back seat and takes in her surroundings. "You live here?" she asks in awe.

"Yes. And now it's your home too."

I park my truck next to the large moving truck, climb out, snag my cut that was lying on the armrest and slip it on. Sydney, who has already hopped out of the back seat, takes in the cut I'm wearing. She then lets her gaze drift over to the five bikes parked in my driveway and my brothers who come filing out of the house. "Holy crap! Are you like a motorcycle club?" The kid doesn't look the least bit concerned at seeing a bunch of big ass bikers standing around my yard. If anything she seems intrigued.

I step beside her and begin introducing everyone. I point to Riggs first. "Sydney, this is Riggs. And standing next to him is his woman, Luna." I watch as Sydney's eyes go big while she watches Riggs communicate with Luna using sign language as he translates our introductions. Next, I motion toward Fender. "This is Fender, then we have Kiwi, Everest, and standing over by the porch is Nova. With him is his daughter Piper."

Sydney continues to take in all the brothers. When her eyes land on a beaming Piper, she smiles. That smile is all the encouragement Piper needs before she rushes down the steps of the porch. "Hi Sydney. As Wick just told you, my name is Piper. Do you want to see your room? I made it up for you. I hope you like it." Piper grabs Sydney's hand and starts leading her inside. I'll admit I was a little worried at how Sydney was going to take being here, but seeing the huge smile on her face as she allows Piper to take her into the house, I'm hoping she will settle in.

"Well," Riggs announces. "Got all the shit unloaded and set up. Josie and Payton went to the grocery store and stocked the refrigerator and cabinets. Piper got the girl's bedroom squared away. She went a bit crazy, but you know how she is. It's gettin' late, so if ya don't mind I'm going to leave the truck here overnight and have one of the guys pick it up in the mornin'."

"No problem, Prez. I appreciate you all steppin' in today and helping my woman and me with Sydney."

Vayda comes to stand beside me. I put my arm around her, pulling her into my side. When she looks up at me with those beautiful fucking eyes that make my dick twitch, I don't hesitate to claim her mouth with mine, right in front of my brothers. Mine and Vayda's public display earns us a round of catcalls. When I look back at them, they are wearing shit-eating grins on their faces.

"You claimin' Tequila, brother?" Riggs asks.

"Yeah, Prez. I'm claimin' my woman."

"Fuck, yeah!" Nova hollers. "It's about fuckin' time you got your head out of your ass."

Vayda is the next to pipe up. "I'll drink to that."

She turns to me to see the annoyed look on my face. "What? It's true. Took your ass long enough."

# 14

# TEQUILA

A couple of days have passed since finding out Damien has a daughter and the same amount of time since bringing her home with us. It's going about as well, or I should say as rough as I expected it to go. "She has hardly stepped foot out of her room since we arrived." Scooping the chopped garlic off the cutting board, I toss it into the skillet with the green beans.

"Give her time. It's a big adjustment. At least she's eating the food you've been taking up to her room." Malik tries reassuring me as he salts the steaks he is about to cook on the grill.

"I guess." Shrugging my shoulders, I turn the fire down on the stove and place the lid on the skillet, letting them simmer. Turning, I take a few steps and lean my hip against the side of the kitchen island. "I can't help but feel a little bummed. I want to get to know my niece. Right now, all I get are resentful glares and short, clipped thank you's." Folding my arms, I sigh.

Stopping what he's doing, Malik reaches out, hooks his finger into the belt loop of my jeans, and pulls me into him. "We've only known her for a few days, but I can tell you with certainty Sydney is a lot like you." He kisses the top of my nose. "Stubborn, strong

151

willed, and determined to do things in her own time on her own terms."

I hate to admit it, but Malik is right. My brother was the same way too. Dipping his head, Malik kisses me just below my ear, sending shivers down my spine, causing my skin to prickle. "Speaking of," he whispers. Lifting his head, he looks beyond my shoulder, and I turn. "I'll be outside." He kisses my temple.

"Hey," I acknowledge Sydney as she shuffles into the kitchen, heading toward the refrigerator.

"Hey." She retrieves a can of soda, then sits on the stool across the counter from me.

Smiling at her, I do my best to interact. "Piper asked about you today. She wants to text you sometime, maybe take you to the mall this weekend. If you're up to it, I could give you her number." At first, all I get out of her is a small shrug of the shoulders.

"Maybe," Sydney finally speaks.

"Great. Hey, listen, you think you could help me with dinner? Those potatoes there," I point to the steaming pile of cooked potatoes in the colander as they drain in the sink, "need to be mashed." I wait for her to respond, but after a few seconds, I tell her, "that's okay. You don't have to. I just thought..."

"Okay." Sydney stands from her seat, and I want to do a victory dance, but I hold in my excitement. Tiny battles won are better than none at all.

"Toss them back in that pot there. You'll find the milk and butter in the refrigerator, and the hand mixer is in that drawer there next to the stove." Going to the freezer side of the refrigerator, I pull out a box of frozen buttered garlic bread. As Sydney gets her things for the mashed potatoes, I dig a cookie sheet out of the cabinet and place the bread on it. "You look like you know your way around a kitchen. Did you help Georgia, I mean, your mom a lot?" I strike up more conversation, hoping she will open up a bit more. Before long, she finally does.

"My mom let me cook all the time." She pours the milk into the pot, then drops butter in it as well. "Um, Vayda?"

"Yeah?" I slide the pan of bread into the oven.

"My mom said I need to get to know you and everything, but," she sighs, "it's tough. I don't know what to do. It feels awkward. The house is nice and everything, but I just don't want to be here." She cuts her eyes at me. "No offense."

I laugh. "None taken." Yep, she's a Wilder alright. Says what's on her mind. No filter. "To tell you the truth, I feel awkward too. I have no idea what I'm doing or how to do it when it comes to kids."

"That's okay. Most days, I have no idea what I'm doing either. Being eleven is not always easy, and as you now know, my life hasn't been typical. Not like some of my friends anyway." She plugs the mixer in and whips the potatoes.

Malik walks into the kitchen, holding the platter of grilled steaks. He looks at Sydney, then to me and mouths "Everything okay?" Nodding, I smile. Nothing more is said as I pull the bread from the oven and begin to plate the food. For the first time since the men furnished the house, we sit down and use the dining table. After fixing her plate, Sydney looks over at Malik and me taking our seats. For a moment, I think she's about to haul ass upstairs back to her bedroom. Instead, she carries her plate to the table, sits down across from me, and starts eating.

"Damn. These potatoes taste amazing. What did you do to them?" Malik shovels another heap into his mouth.

"Nothing. Sydney made them." I tell him and watch Sydney peek up from her plate at Malik.

"No, shit? Eleven years old and you can cook like this? I don't know what you put in it, but I love em'." Malik smiles at her and takes another bite.

For the first time, Sydney cracks a small smile. Not much of one, but enough to know she has my brother's smile. "It's the sour cream. My mom's secret to the world's best mashed potatoes." Just as fast as she smiles, her face falls, and she pushes her food around on her plate. "I miss her."

"She happen to tell you when she would call?" I ask.

"She can't call for another week. Something about no phone privileges during the first two weeks." She stares at her plate. "Stupid rules," she mumbles.

"As soon as she can have visitors, we'll go see your mom," Malik mentions as he cuts his steak, causing Sydney to look at him, her mouth gaped open, and her eyes wide.

"You would do that—for me?" she says, shocked by his offer.

"Yeah." He looks at her. "You're family. We take care of each other. You want to see your mom; then, we will make it happen. Simple as that." When my niece looks at me, I nod.

The rest of the dinner is spent in silence. Once Sydney finishes her food, she rinses her plate. "I'm kind of tired."

"There's ice cream for dessert if you want some," I offer, while I clean the kitchen.

"I don't want any." Sydney turns around to leave the kitchen but stops. "Vayda, Malik. Thanks." She never looks back before exiting the kitchen, and we hear her footsteps as she climbs the stairs.

"Here." Malik hands me a glass filled with whiskey.

"Thanks." I take it from him. The taste of bourbon is sweet as it coats my tongue. Malik comes up behind me, kisses my neck, and I close my eyes.

"You ever thought about kids? Having one of your own that is?"

That's an out of the blue question. Nevertheless, I think about it for a second. I mean, sure I've thought about it. In passing, but not as often as one would think a woman would. "My life hasn't slowed down enough to give it much thought. Besides, what I do for a living doesn't necessarily scream motherhood."

He kisses my neck again. This time his tongue grazes my skin.

"A lot of women soldiers balance their military career with family. They do it every day."

Taking another sip, I lean my head to one side, as Malik continues to pepper kisses on my skin. The smell of his woodsy cologne mixed with the scent of his leather cut and whiskey breath fills my senses. It's intoxicating. "Do you want kids?" I groan.

"I do." He sits his drink on the counter and spins my body to face him. "With you." His eyes bore into mine, and suddenly I find it hard to breathe.

Then I kiss him.

His tongue tangles with mine as he grabs hold of my ass and lifts me onto the counter. His hands run up my bare thighs. Spreading my legs, he steps between them. We make out like we're a couple of teenagers, before he pulls away, leaving us both gasping for air and wanting more. "We're taking this to the room." Malik pulls my ass to the very edge of the counter and presses his hard cock against my eager center. Shamelessly, I grind against him. Leaving our drinks on the counter, Malik lifts me. Wrapping my legs over his hips, he carries me up the stairs. I kiss him, just behind his ear, and he groans. Walking down the hallway, I glance at Sydney's bedroom door. "What about Sydney?" Malik steps into our bedroom, closing the door, then presses my back against it. He grinds into me. "Are you a screamer, baby?"

"Something like that," I pant.

Malik carries me to the bed and lays me down. "Guess you'll have to keep that pretty mouth of yours shut." Grabbing the hem of my shirt, Malik lifts the fabric up and over my head. "Fuck, you're perfect." He cups both breasts, squeezing them, then drags his palms down my sides, stopping when he skims over the sports tape covering my ribcage. "Shit. I wasn't thinkin'. Maybe we should wait."

"Oh, hell no. You better finish what you started."

"You sure?"

Reaching down, I palm his erection, rubbing his cock through his jeans, showing him how sure I am. "Fuck me, Malik."

That's all it takes. Unbuttoning my shorts, Malik slides them down my long legs, taking my panties with them, and tosses them to the floor. Exposed to him, Malik steps back. "I'll be gentle, baby." Not breaking our connection, he shrugs his cut off, tossing it to the bench at the foot of the bed. Peeling his shirt off, he does the same. Sinking to the floor, Malik wraps his hands around my calf, pulling me to the edge of the bed. He parts my legs. "Your pussy already wet for me, baby?" He draws me even closer, placing one bent knee over his shoulder then doing the same with the other. "I'm going to taste you before I fuck you, Vayda."

I look down at him, wanting to watch him take his first taste of me. Dipping his head between my thighs, he holds my stare as he swipes his tongue up my center. The moment he sucks my clit into his mouth I throw my head back on a moan, and my legs quiver. Gripping the blanket beneath me and biting my lip, I stifle my need to scream. "I'm so close." My hips rise, pressing into his face, my body desperate to come. My orgasm builds, and my legs start to quiver again. Just as I'm about to fall over the edge, Malik stops. "No-no-no. What are you doing?" I reach for him as he stands.

"As good as your pussy tastes, I want you to come with my cock buried deep inside you," he says as he rids himself of the rest of his clothes. Feeling dirty, and horny as hell, I position myself in the middle of his bed. Reaching between my thighs I rub my swollen clit. I throw my head back as I pleasure myself in front of him. When I look back at Malik, he's stroking his large cock as he watches me. My orgasm starts to build again, so I pick up speed. "That orgasm is mine." He growls and advances on me. The bed dips as he brings his body over mine, then captures my mouth with his. It's during this kiss he settles between my legs, lines the head of his cock up at my entrance and stops. "You protected?"

"Yes."

As soon as the word leaves my mouth he slowly sinks into me.

I gasp as my body adjusts to his size. He stops.

"Don't stop." I grip his ass and tighten my hips around him.

"Easy, baby." Malik dips his head, taking my nipple in his mouth and I whimper. His attention to my body doesn't relent. He licks and nips, giving each breast equal attention. "I swear, I'll never get enough of you."

"That's a good thing, because I'll never get enough of you either," I breathe, spreading my legs wider as he guides his cock in and out of me. I slide my hands up his sides, over his shoulders, down his chest until my fingers find the grooves of his well defined abs.

"Fuck. You're so wet, and tight." Malik continues his torturous pace. He thrusts into me going deeper and deeper bringing me closer to the edge.

"I'm close," I pant digging my nails into his back as my toes curl and my walls begin to pulse.

Sliding his hand underneath me, Malik grabs hold of my ass, bringing us closer together. He's on a mission to imprint himself on me; in me like no other man before him has. He is determined to leave his mark.

"Mine," he growls. "Every single inch of you belongs to me."

"Yes. Only you."

Releasing his hold on my ass, Malik brings his hand up, cupping my breast. Leaning down, he feasts on my nipple which has a direct line to my pussy.

"Come for me, baby. Let me feel your pussy come all over my cock."

His demand sends me over the edge and my center clamps down around his length as he plants himself deep inside me, taking him with me. We hold onto each other as our combined climax surges through our bodies. I have never experienced a moment more powerful than this one. We lay in bed together, neither one of us speaking. We're content just being in the moment together. Just as I feel myself starting to fall asleep, rapid gunfire breaks the stillness of the night. Glass shatters as bullets hit the windowpane, sounding the house alarm. On instinct, I roll from the bed to the floor, covering my head and reaching for my weapon that normally would be laying beside me on the nightstand, but of course it isn't there. My sore ribs immediately begin to throb from slamming into the wood floor.

Suddenly Malik's massive body is covering mine. In his right hand he's holding his handgun. Sydney's blood-curdling scream raises the hairs on my arms, and before I have time to think, I'm out from under Malik and running out of the bedroom. Bursting through Sydney's bedroom door at the end of the hall, I find her huddled between her bed and the wall. On the other side of her bed the windowpane is shattered and broken glass is scattered across her bed. I rush to her side, kneeling beside her. Only when she looks at me then drops her eyes do I realize I'm still naked.

"What's happening?" she yells, covering her ears.

"I don't know, but you need to stay low. Crawl on your hands and knees to my room!" I yell back at her, but she's frozen with fear, and she doesn't attempt to move. "Sydney. You need to trust me," I plead, and she nods. "Good. Now move. I'm right behind you." We come across Malik, waiting right outside the bedroom door. He has his pants, boots, and cut on already. Phone in one hand and weapon in the other. "You have an extra one of those for me?" I gesture to his gun.

"Put some fuckin' clothes on first. We need to leave," he says with urgency. Without question, I crawl into the room, find my discarded clothes on the floor, and throw them on.

"Vayda. Why is someone shooting at the house?" Sydney

doesn't move far from my side as I sit on my ass and slip my shoes on my feet.

"No time for questions, sweetheart." Realizing she's barefoot, I reach for my other pair of boots sitting by the dresser and put them on her feet. "No matter what happens, you stay right behind me, and don't let go of my hand, got it?" Sydney nods again, the fear in her eyes making me question if I should have brought her to Louisiana at all. "I won't let anything happen to you. I promise." I take hold of her hand.

"Stay close," Malik orders as he leads us down the hall. He pauses just before taking the first step on the staircase, and peers over the railing. Once he's sure it's safe to descend, with our backs pressed against the wall, we make our way down. The instant we've cleared the stairs, and are standing in the foyer, another round of bullets hit the house, shattering the stained-glass window pane above the front door. "Get to the garage!" Malik yells above the deafening sound of the house alarm.

Punching in his code, Malik unlocks the door to the garage, and we rush to his truck. Flinging the backdoor open I usher Sydney inside. "Lay as flat as you can on the floorboard," I command, and she tucks herself into the fetal position behind the passenger seat as low as she can go. I climb in behind her as Malik jumps in behind the wheel. Flipping the visor down, a set of spare keys drop into his palm. He fires up the engine and makes eye contact with me in the rearview mirror as the garage door begins to rise.

"Hold on."

**15**

**WICK**

Sydney screams from the backseat of my truck where Vayda uses her own body to shield her niece. "Aunt Vayda, what's happening?" Sydney's voice rings out full of fear.

"We're going to be okay, sweetheart. Malik is going to get us somewhere safe." Vayda says that statement with confidence.

"You two hang on. We're almost to the clubhouse." I continue to navigate the streets, purposely taking wrong turns to ensure we are not followed back to the clubhouse. Just as I conclude we are not being tailed, I'm proven wrong when a single headlight appears in my rearview mirror, and the sound of a motorcycle penetrates the air around us. I can tell immediately it's not one of my brothers. It doesn't take long for the bike to eat up the distance between them and us. "Fuck," I curse under my breath.

Digging my cell from my pocket, I dial Riggs. The phone rings several times before going straight to voicemail. "Shit."

Next, I dial Nova. His phone rings and rings, before it too goes to voicemail. *What the fuck is happening? It's not like my brothers to not answer their phones. Something is not right.*

Next, I try Fender. He answers on the second ring. "Yeah?"

"Fender!" I bark into the phone.

Fender is now alert. "What's goin' on, Wick?" I hear a rustling noise over the phone.

"Someone just shot up my fuckin' house, man."

"What the fuck! Are you guys, okay? Where are you now? I'm walking out of the clubhouse now." Fender says just before I hear a pounding and Kiwi's voice in the background.

"I just turned right on Bower. I tried callin', Prez, and Nova. Neither one answered their phone. That shit is not sittin' right with me. I want you to check on Riggs and Luna. Tell Kiwi I said to see about Nova and Piper. And tell Everest to meet me at the gate but stay vigilant. I'm two minutes out, and I got some guy hot on my ass."

"Do you want backup?'

"No. I can handle this motherfucker. Just get to Riggs and Nova so we can see what the hell is goin' on."

"You got it, Wick." Fender affirms, and the line goes dead.

"What is it, Malik?" Vayda asks as she lifts her head to peek over the back seat behind us.

"Stay down!" I shout the same moment the back window shatters, sending shards of broken glass flying everywhere.

"Shit!" Vayda hisses. "I thought it was one of the guys."

"Vayda, I need you to get this son of a bitch off my ass."

Leaning over, I open the glove compartment, and retrieve the gun I keep in there. Vayda reaches up toward the front seat and takes the weapon from me. "Take that motherfucker out, baby."

With skilled movement, Vayda rises to her knees, braces her back against the back of my seat, aims the gun, and takes the shot. My girl hits her mark on the first try. The bike behind us immediately goes down. The guy riding it eats asphalt as his body hits the pavement where he skids across the street. Vayda turns to look at me. "I got your six. Get us the hell out of here."

A minute later, I fly through the gate of the clubhouse. Everest is there waiting on us, his weapon in his hand. I jump out of the truck and fling the back door open to reveal a scared and crying Sydney. "Baby," I address Vayda, who climbs out of the back seat and begins coaxing her niece out. "I need you to take Sydney inside." Those words barely leave my mouth when the sound of a motorcycle has me shoving Vayda and Sydney behind me and drawing my pistol on the person speeding through the gate of the clubhouse. I lower my weapon when I see it's Nova and Piper. Nova pulls his bike up next to my truck as Kiwi roars in behind him. The look on Nova's face is pure murder. Piper, on the other hand, is shaking like a leaf and has tears in her eyes.

"Someone took shots at my house," Nova seethes.

"My place was just shot up, too," I tell him.

"Are you fuckin' serious, brother?"

I shake my head. "I wish I wasn't."

Nova looks around. "Is my brother here? He wasn't answering my calls."

"No. I sent Fender over to the bar to check on him and Luna. He didn't answer my call either."

Nova and I share a look. It only takes two seconds for the situation to click. "Fuck. We need to go."

Jumping into action, I turn back to Vayda. "Can you take Sydney and Piper inside? Nova and I need to go check on Riggs and Luna."

Vayda nods and ushers the two girls inside without question. I then turn and bark my orders at Everest and Kiwi. "You two stay here with the women. Vayda took one guy out on the way here, but we don't know who we are dealing with and how many. I don't want to take any chances by leaving the women without protection." Both men give me a chin lift.

"Be safe," Everest calls out as I hop back into my truck, and Nova mounts his bike. Nova follows behind me as I peel out of the clubhouse parking lot and head in the direction of Twisted

Throttle. The streets of New Orleans are eerily quiet as Nova, and I pull up in front of the bar next to Fender's bike. My eyes zero in on the bar's busted-out window. There is also the distinct smell of gasoline and smoke. I rush through the broken entrance door finding Fender with a fire extinguisher in his hand. "Where are Prez and Luna?"

"Right here, brother," Riggs answers me as he walks through the back-double doors at the far corner of the bar with Luna in tow. "I want to get Luna the fuck out of here now. We can worry about the bar later. Let's roll," Riggs grinds out. I know the look on his face all too well. He's out for blood. Well, he can join the club, because blood is the only form of payment I'll be accepting for what went down tonight.

Back at the clubhouse, my brothers and I hold church. I'm halfway through my cigarette when Riggs finally speaks. "Tonight, our homes and our families were targeted. Wick and Nova's houses were riddled with bullets, whereas the bar was deliberately set on fire. Right now, I am not concerned about the damage. What's important is we are all okay, and everyone is safe. It goes without sayin' we are on lockdown. That means I don't want Luna, Piper, Sydney, Josie, Payton or Zara leaving the clubhouse. I don't want them to so much as step one foot outside." Riggs looks at me. "I'm not including Tequila in the lockdown because I know how she is at takin' orders. Someone came after her niece, so she'll be out for vengeance. It will be up to you as to how you want to handle your woman." I give Riggs a chin lift. Vayda is not like the other women here. She has military training and the same skill sets as me. Vayda operates the same as we do. There will be no keeping her on lockdown.

The sound of Kiwi tapping away on his laptop at the end of the table draws my attention. "You have anything for us, man?"

"I'm pulling up the street cam across from the bar now." He taps a few more keys. "Motherfucker," he bites out.

"What you got?" Riggs asks.

Kiwi looks up from his computer. "Cameras across the street from the bar got a guy wearin' a Los Demonios cut tossin' a Molotov cocktail through the window of Twisted Throttle. Cameras tracked him slithering around toward the back of the bar. About thirty seconds later he's seen exiting the alley on his bike. That's when Fender comes into view."

I ask Fender, who's sitting beside me. "What did you see when you arrived?"

"I saw the assholes retreating tail lights as I rode up. I chose to let him go when I saw the broken-out window and the fire. That's when I kicked in the entrance door, went behind the bar where I know Prez keeps a fire extinguisher and put the fire out."

"Here," Kiwi says, turning on the big screen TV mounted on the wall. A second later the footage of what went down at the bar plays out. I clenched my fist when I watch a Los Demonios try to burn down mine and Riggs' bar with him and his pregnant woman inside. Then we all watch as Fender pulls up on his bike, hops off and kicks the door in. Kiwi then swaps the footage out to the cameras we have in the bar. Just as Fender puts the fire out, Riggs comes flying down the stairs with his gun drawn.

Riggs clears his throat as he addresses Fender. "You had mine and Luna's back tonight, brother. Thank you."

Fender tips his head. "Always, Prez."

We all take a moment to reflect on how lucky we are that nobody was killed tonight before I speak again. "What's the plan, Prez? I've been out of town dealin' with my own personal shit; I never got the chance to ask if you talked to Jake about Los Demonios."

"I talked to Jake after we got back from the event. I told him what went down. To say he was livid would be an understatement. As far as he knew Los Demonios had stayed out of the states. When his club took down the fuckers that set up residence in

Montana a couple of years back, the main charter heeded Jake's warning and has been layin' low ever since. Jake offered to be of service. He and his men are on stand-by if we should require additional manpower."

"Why now, though, Prez?" This comes from Kiwi. "Why are Los Demonios showin' their arses now? Things just aren't addin' up. I understand them wanting to retaliate after what happened at the rally, but what I'm questioning is why they were at the rally in the first place."

"I'm with Kiwi on this one," I add. "My gut is tellin' me them showin' up is somehow linked to what went down in Mexico."

Riggs takes in my statement. "You thinkin' Cortez and Los Demonios are connected?"

"I'm thinkin' we need to find out, explore all possible avenues. I also want to question Zara again. The first time we spoke with her about Cortez, Los Demonios wasn't a part of the equation. I say we question her again."

Riggs turns his attention from me to Everest. "Go get Zara and bring her in here."

Everest does as he's told and goes to retrieve Zara. He returns moments later with her. She walks into the room with hesitating steps as she wrings her hands together in front of her body. Riggs is quick to assure her. "It's alright darlin'. We want to ask you a couple of questions."

Zara visibly swallows. "S...sure."

Riggs points to the TV on the wall where Kiwi has enlarged a still shot of the asshole Los Demonios who tried to burn the bar down tonight. The image is only a side profile of his face, but there is no mistaking the club emblem on his cut. "Do you recognize this man?"

Zara loses all color in her face. "Th...that's Carlito. He's the president of Los Demonios, a club from Mexico. He's also my husband's brother."

Zara starts to shake uncontrollably. "He's found us, hasn't he? Please! You can't let him take my son."

I go to stand in front of Zara. "What did we tell you when we first brought you here?"

"You said you and your club would protect my son and me."

"That's right, sweetheart. My brothers and I won't let anything happen to you and your boy."

Zara's shoulders drop, and she loses some of her tension. I nod to Everest. He escorts her back out of the room, and I take my seat back at the table. Riggs looks down at his watch.

"With it being' nearly two in the mornin', I say we hunker down for a bit. Come sunup; we roll out. Kiwi and Fender, I want the two of you to double-check the clubhouse perimeter along with the motion sensors and alarms before turnin' in for the night. Nova, you go check on Piper. And Wick, make sure Sydney is settled. The kid witnessed some heavy shit earlier. That on top of what she's already going through has probably taken its toll." With nothing left to say, Riggs slams the gavel.

The guys and I file out of church, and I head straight to my room here at the clubhouse. Though Vayda has a room here, I know she'll be in mine. I'm proven right when I open the door to see her standing in front of the window, staring out. She turns her head when the door clicks shut behind me. "Where is Sydney?" I ask.

"She's down the hall in my room with Piper. The two have really taken to each other. Piper has a way of settling Sydney. I checked on them ten minutes ago. They finally fell asleep."

"That's good." I stride toward where Vayda is standing. She turns to me immediately and snakes her arms around my waist. Her arm brushing against my side causes me to wince. Vayda notices and pulls back. Lifting my cut, she takes in my bloody tee. "What the hell, Malik!" She tugs my shirt up over my ribcage. "Oh my god! You've been shot!"

"Bullet only grazed me, baby. I'm fine."

"You didn't think to tell somebody?" Vayda grabs my hand and leads me into the bathroom. "I'm going to clean you up."

Opening the cabinet beneath the sink, Vayda grabs the first aid kit. She pulls out rubbing alcohol, sterile gauze, ointment, and lays the items out on the counter. The whole time she's grumbling under her breath. "I can't believe you got shot and didn't say anything."

"It's not that bad, baby. I doubt it even needs stitches."

"Not the point, Malik," Vayda throws her arms up exasperated. She's so fucking cute when she gets riled up. And before she can go to say another word, I snake my arm around her waist, pulling her body flush against mine. "I love it when you get all hot. Makes my dick so fuckin' hard." I press my cock against her stomach, letting her feel just how much she affects me. "Give me that sassy mouth of yours." I don't wait for a response before my mouth comes crashing down on hers. Fuck. Every kiss from Vayda is like a breath of fresh air. This woman has no clue what she does to me.

Too soon, we break apart, and she goes about cleaning me up. As expected, the bullet only grazed me. No stitches required. After slathering some ointment and placing a bandage over the wound, Vayda and I crawl into bed where I tuck my woman into my side as she lays her head on my chest.

"You going to tell me what you and the guys talked about downstairs?"

"Nope."

Vayda leans up on her elbow. "Malik? You don't expect me to be the kind of woman who sits back while the men handle business, do you?" She narrows her eyes, and I can't help but chuckle.

"Fuck no. I know that's not the kind of woman you are. I wouldn't have you any other way either. No matter how big a pain in the ass you are."

"Excuse me?" Vayda goes to dole out a tongue lashing, but I'm quick to cut her off.

"You know I can't discuss what goes down in church between me and my brothers. That's somethin' you're going to have to respect." I level her with a look that leaves no room for argument. This is not something I will negotiate on, and she knows it.

"I can tell you the women are on lockdown—all of them but you. Riggs has already said the lockdown doesn't apply to you. My brothers know and respect the kind of person you are and how seriously you take your duty to protect others." I cup Vayda's cheek as I speak my next words. "I would never hinder who you are or your calling in life, Vayda. And neither would my club. You are a strong, independent, fierce woman. You have dedicated years of your life not only to your country but to anyone who needs help. Tonight, someone has gone after the people you love, and like me, you will not rest until you have served your brand of justice. As much as I want to lock you away and shelter you from the dangers of the underworld, I can't. I would be taking away who you are."

# 16

# TEQUILA

Covering his hand with mine, I let Malik's words sink in. Once again, he renders me speechless. Leaning down, he presses his lips hard against mine once more, solidifying the fact, he meant every word. Malik gently pulls me on top of him, and I instantly regret my decision to wear my clothes to bed, because I didn't want to be caught off guard again. I rock my body against his, creating friction between us. "Lose the clothes," he demands. I'm in the middle of removing my shirt when a soft knock on the door halts everything. Undeterred, Malik unfastens the button on my jeans. "Go away," he growls.

"Aunt Vayda," Sydney calls from the other side of the bedroom door.

Pulling my shirt down, I roll off of Malik, back to my side of the bed, and lean against the headboard. Reaching over, I turn the lamp beside the bed on. "You can come in," I tell her, and the door slowly opens. An unsure Sydney steps inside and looks from me to Malik.

"Um." Her eyes settle on me, and I smile at her.

"Have you seen my phone? I had it in my pajamas pocket

before we left the house, and now I can't find it." She picks at a loose thread on the hem of her shirt.

"Sweetheart, it's late. I thought you were asleep." Sydney's eyes drop to the floor. I sigh. Hell, I can't even fall asleep, why would I expect her to be able to? Especially after what she's been through tonight. "I tell you what. It may be in Malik's truck." I glance over at Malik, who has his arms crossed behind his head as he listens.

Sydney's eyes dart to Malik. "Can I go look?" she asks, hopeful.

"No," Malik says a bit too harshly, and Sydney flinches. I narrow my eyes on him. "I don't mean to be an ass, but one; no one is allowed outside the clubhouse right now. Two; it's 2:00 am. You should be in bed, getting some sleep," Malik explains, and Sydney crosses her arms and stares him down, clearly not happy with being told no, or what to do for that matter.

It makes me think of someone else I know. *Me.*

"I'll see if I can go outside and look for it myself. Okay?" Climbing out of bed, I cross the room, and wrap my arms around her. She stiffens for a second before melting into my embrace. "Why do you need your phone?"

Sydney sighs. "I'm worried I may miss a text or call from my mom," she admits.

After all she has been through, her only concern is for her mom. Not once since the entire ordeal took place, and her life was in danger, has Sydney complained. She has had her world turned upside down in more ways than one over the past week and has taken it all in stride. I stroke her hair. "If we don't find your phone, I'll get you a new one. Until then, your mom has my number and your granddad's. If she can't contact you, she can always contact one of us."

Sydney's arms wrap around my waist, hugging me back. "Okay," she mumbles, sounding somewhat satisfied.

"There you are." A sleepy Piper appears in the doorway. "I woke up, and you were gone."

"Why don't you go back to bed?" I coax Sydney, who seems to forget all about her phone, for now, and follows Piper back to their room.

"I didn't mean to be so harsh," Malik mentions as I settle down beside him. "There's a fire in that one. I have a feeling she has a thing about authority and following rules."

I grin, knowing he's right. "I can only imagine what must be going through her head right now." I turn the lamp off, and Malik pulls me into his side. "She worries too much for an eleven-year old, and now I've gone and added to it by bringing her here," I admit. "I could never forgive myself if something happens to her. She's a part of my brother. I can't lose her too. She could have been shot tonight, Malik."

"I won't let anything happen to the two of you. I swear it."

"I believe you." I rest my head on his shoulder, both of us resting but never falling asleep.

I'm not sure how much time passes as I lay in bed, staring at the ceiling, but it feels like forever. The room is basked in darkness. The only light filtering in through the room is coming from a crack in the curtains hanging on the window. How are we supposed to sleep knowing someone is out there wanting to harm the club? What's worse is knowing they are willing to harm women and children in the process. None of which should surprise me knowing who could be behind the attacks on all the club members tonight.

Still feeling wound up and uneasy, I throw the covers off my body. Pulling away from Malik's embrace, I sit on the side of the bed. "Where are you running off to?" he asks, his voice alert.

"I'm not running. I just need to look in on the girls one more time." Still fully dressed, minus my boots, I stand and grab my gun from the nightstand. Hearing the cover shuffle, I look back, and Malik has his back pressed against the headboard.

"You're safe here, Vayda," Malik watches me clip the holster to my waistband. "Sorry. Habit." I cross the room. "I'll be right back," I tell him and exit the bedroom.

The clubhouse is eerily silent, and I pause, thinking I heard a noise. Standing stock-still, I listen for a moment, only hearing myself breathing and conclude I'm letting my nerves get the better of me. Usually, I'm not like this. Paranoid. Maybe being responsible for the well being of my niece now is what's making me leerier. Perhaps that is also why I keep having these sick feelings in the pit of my stomach that something is not right in the first place. I've never been responsible for anyone other than myself unless outside my usual line of work.

Continuing down the hall, I grab a hold of the knob to the room Sydney and Piper are sleeping in, and turn. Cracking the door open, I peek inside, finding Piper in the twin bed closest to the door. Opening the door a little further, I glance to the other side of the room, finding the other bed empty. Walking farther into the room, I see no sign of her. Crossing the floor, I rub Piper on the shoulder, waking her. She rolls slightly on her back.

"Vayda?" Piper rubs her eyes, trying to focus on my face.

"Piper, where is Sydney?" I ask her, trying not to panic.

"Um. She was asleep before I dozed off. Maybe she woke up needing to go to the bathroom." Piper offers a reasonable explanation because their room doesn't have its own private bathroom. If they needed to go, they would have to walk down to the end of the hall. "You want me to go see?" Piper asks and goes to sit up in bed.

"No, Sweetie, that's okay. I'll go. Try to go back to sleep." Leaving the bedroom, I close the door and make my way to the end of the hall. The bathroom door is closed, but I notice no light is shining from beneath the door. Knocking softly, I whisper her name, trying not to disturb anyone else nearby. "Sydney?" No answer. Opening the door, I find the bathroom empty. I flip the switch on the wall, but the light doesn't come on. I flip it on and off a couple of more times, getting the same results.

"Everything okay?" Malik's deep timber from behind startles me, and I turn around, ready to swing. "Woah, it's just me, baby. What's got you so damn jumpy?"

"Dammit, Malik. Don't sneak up on me like that; I could have hurt you." I lower my fisted hand to my side. It's dark as hell in the unlit hallway, but I can hear the amusement of my comment in his voice when he grabs my hand.

"Really?" Malik pulls me into his body.

"Sydney isn't in her room, Malik. I thought maybe she would have gone to the bathroom, but she isn't here either." I tell him.

Keeping hold of my hand, he tells me. "Come on, let's check downstairs. Maybe she couldn't sleep and found her way to the kitchen or somethin'." He tugs on my hand and leads me down the hall to the stairs. "There's no lights downstairs." He observes as we descend. At the base of the steps, Malik turns to his right, feeling along the wall for the light switches. I hear him flick them a few times, and nothing happens. "Shit, light must be blown."

"The lights were not working in the bathroom upstairs," I add.

"Could be the breaker then. The damn thing trips from time to time. I'm going to the back to check it out. You head into the kitchen and see if Sydney is in there." Malik informs me, and he heads toward the back near the small storage room, and I head into the kitchen.

Just for kicks, I check the lights, and not surprised they don't come on either. The kitchen is small, and what little moonlight that is shining through a couple of small windows lining the wall above the sink, I can make out most of my surroundings. Sydney isn't here. My stomach sinks and my gut tells me something isn't right. Rushing out of the kitchen, my eyes dart around the darkened room where the bar and pool tables are. I dash toward the couch sitting against the wall, hoping I'll find her curled up on the cushions. My head whips to the side when I hear the creaking of a door, and a gust of wind brushes my arm. The front door to the clubhouse is cracked open. *Shit.* I run to the door, fling it open, and call out her name. "Sydney!" My heart races against my chest as panic sets in. Gravel crunches beneath my feet as I rush out into the open yard, finding no one.

Looking up, I notice the light that usually illuminates the property isn't working. It's pitch black out here besides the glow from the moon casting it's light on the Mississippi River that flows several yards to the left of me. I catch a flash out of the corner of my eye. Looking to my right, I see nothing but Malik's truck. That's when I notice the passenger door on the driver's side is hanging open. Pulling my gun from the holster strapped to my hip, I flip the safety and slowly advance in the direction of the vehicle. When I make it to the open door, my barefoot steps on a smooth object. Before looking down and without removing my foot, I peer inside the back of the truck, finding it empty as well. Checking my surroundings, I then squat. A dim light shining lets me know I stepped on a cellphone. Picking it up, I realize it's Sydney's. I had told her I would grab it for her but forgot. The screen lights up again, with a notification of a new text message. Something inside me causes my thumb to swipe the screen, and tap the notification icon. The moment I do, my heart sinks to my stomach at the image on the screen—Sydney's frightened tear-stained face as she sits on a dirty floor. Below the text image is a message.

*You have something that belongs to me.*

*My son for the girl.*

*You have until sunrise, or you'll find pieces of her floating down the river.*

*By the way, you can keep the whore.*

I take off toward the clubhouse, with the phone clutched in one hand and my weapon still in the other, crashing through the partially opened door, causing it to slam hard against the wall behind it. "Malik!" My lungs burn at how loud I scream his name.

Suddenly the lights in the clubhouse come on, and just as Malik runs into the room, I hear a commotion upstairs and stomping feet running down the stairs. "What?" Malik is at my side. "Did you find Sydney?"

I shake my head, holding my emotions back, and hand him the phone. "She isn't here." My voice cracks, and I feel like I'm about to lose my shit. By this time, Riggs, Nova, Kiwi, and Fender rush over.

"What the hell is going on down here?" Riggs demands, standing in nothing but a pair of jeans. Malik's face hardens as he stares at the screen.

I look at Riggs. "Cortez has Sydney."

"How the fuck did they get your niece?" he questions, and I rush to explain my theory.

"I went to check on her and Piper, but she wasn't in her bed. Then I checked the bathroom, and the kitchen while Malik was checking the breaker box in the supply room. I found the front door barely cracked open. When I ventured outside, I noticed Malik's truck door ajar. Thinking Sydney may have gone out to find her cellphone, I investigated. Her phone was lying on the ground." Tears sting my eyes as they threaten to break free. "There's an image of Sydney on her phone. With a message from Cortez. He wants a trade. His son for my niece." I swallow hard past the lump in my throat. Malik takes hold of my hand, giving me support.

Riggs scrubs his palm down his face. "Shit." And Nova rushes up the stairs informing everyone along the way he is going to check on his daughter. The room falls silent, just for a split second, before Zara has our undivided attention.

"You can't have him." Zara cries, holding her sleeping son in one arm, while her other hand trembles as she aims a gun in our direction. *Where the hell did she get a gun?*

"Take it easy." Kiwi takes a step in her direction, and she points the gun at him. He stops, putting his hands out in front of himself. "We're not going to hurt you." He tries assuring her, but she's not listening.

"Don't come any closer. I don't want to shoot anyone, but I will if I have to." Tears stream down her face.

"Whose firearm did she get a hold of?" Riggs asks, not taking his eyes off Zara.

"Mine." Kiwi answers. "It's the one I keep in the top drawer of my nightstand."

"And, I'm assuming it's loaded?" Riggs looks for clarification.

"Yep," Kiwi confirms.

The sound of bare feet slapping against the steps causes all our heads to turn and find Luna walking down the stairs. Luna's hands lift, singing something, before turning her head, finding Zara with a gun in her hand. Luna's eyes widen with fear.

"Upstairs. Now!" Riggs yells as he signs his warning, then speaks to Zara, as Luna rushes back up the stairs. "Listen to me. We will figure all this out. Now, give Kiwi the gun." Zara darts her eyes from Riggs to Kiwi, who is standing closer than the rest of us.

Her head shakes violently. "No. My son and I mean nothing to you and your club. I can't trust anyone. It's up to me to keep my son out of the hands of that monster." While saying this, I notice Nova slowly making his way down the stairs behind Zara, pausing on every step, trying to be as quiet as possible. He lifts his finger, pressing it to his lips.

I take a few steps to the left. My movement has Zara swinging the gun in my direction. I try my best to not only distract her but convince her once more that The Kings would never give her son to Cortez. "Zara." Malik takes a step toward me, causing Zara to divert her eyes to him. Worried, she may get too jumpy and pull the trigger, I grab her attention again. "Zara," I say a bit firmer, and her eyes dart back to me, the gun still pointing at the men. "We are here to help you. I promise you they will keep Julian safe." Zara's body shudders as she begins to cry harder. "Trust us and put down the gun."

At a standoff, we wait for Zara to make her choice, and hope like hell someone doesn't get hurt before it ends. Zara's arm falls to her side, her finger still on the trigger, giving Nova the opportunity he needs to rush in and quickly disarm her. Backing herself into the nearest corner with her son still in her arms, Zara sinks to her knees in defeat. "Vayda, I am so sorry," she cries. "I never meant for any of this to happen. I'm only thinking of my son. I want him to have a better life. One free of crime and evil."

Amidst the chaos that continues to erupt around me, and worried for my own family, I kneel on the floor in front of her. I understand her desperation and the willingness to go to any extreme to keep her child safe. I know now, I would do the same for Sydney. Zara looks at me. "You'll have to kill him. It's the only way to make him stop."

I brush the curls atop her little boy's head, who is still fast asleep in her arms as she sobs uncontrollably. Then, glance over my shoulder, seeking Malik, finding him across the room. My eyes connect with his, and I know without a shadow of doubt Malik and The Kings will get Sydney back. "Make no mistake; death is coming for Cortez," I tell Zara with absolution.

**17**

# WICK

I watch Vayda from across the room as she does her best to console Zara. Not only has Sydney been taken by Cortez, but Zara had gotten it in her head we'd turn her and her son over to her husband and decided to go fucking nuclear on the club by threating to unload a clip on our asses. The woman has some balls, that's for damn sure. I can't even blame her for her actions. She's a mother. Zara reacted in a way any mother would in that situation. And though I understand the woman, I'm unable to hide my irritation. "Everest!" I thunder, my voice echoing off the walls of the clubhouse. "Take Zara back to her room with her son and lock them in." My words clipped, and my tone harsh. I don't miss the look Vayda tosses over her shoulder at me as she passes Zara off to Everest. I know she thinks I'm an ass, but while dealing with Zara, we wasted precious time that could have been spent figuring out where Sydney is.

"Church," Riggs barks. "Tequila, you can join us."

Vayda doesn't have to be told twice. She steps to my side, and we file into church. I drag an extra seat from the corner of the room and pull it up beside me then motion for Vayda to take a

178

seat. Once Everest and Kiwi join us, Riggs gets down to business. "I would start by askin' how the fuck Cortez and his men were able to gain access to our property. Let alone cut our goddamn power considering my orders were to double-check every fuckin' thing hours ago but we don't have time for that shit." Prez levels Kiwi with a hard stare. "I'll be wanting those answers later. For now, pull up the photo of Sydney." Prez tosses Sydney's cell to Kiwi. Kiwi wastes no time connecting the phone to his laptop. His fingers glide across the keyboard of his computer at a rapid pace. Seconds later the photo taken of Sydney appears on the TV over Riggs' shoulder. Out the corner of my eye I gauge Vayda's reaction. Not surprisingly, there is none. She sits quietly in the chair beside me, her expression not giving away a thing and her body language, stiff. Anyone who didn't know Vayda would think she is almost bored, but that's not the case at all. I take in the vein pulsing on her neck and the way her eyes are glued to the TV screen where a photo of her frightened niece is displayed. She's scanning the picture looking for the same thing the rest of us are; clues. It takes me all of three seconds to spot one.

Standing, I stride over to the TV and point to the top left corner of the photo. "Zoom in right there, Kiwi." It's faint but it's there. The top half of a pointed metal roof. "This is the control tower over at the train yard."

As soon as the words leave my mouth, the chair Vayda is sitting in scrapes across the floor. "We need to go." She races for the door.

"Not so fast," Riggs calls out, halting her movements.

"You know that's not how this is going to work, baby," I cut in. "We don't go in without a plan."

"Yeah? Well, you all can sit around and waste time while you come up with that plan. I'm going to get my niece back." Vayda turns her back and heads for the door.

"Get your ass back here."

My words cause Vayda to stop in her tracks. She turns to me with murder in her eyes. I hear Riggs mummer *fuck* next to me

"What did you say?"

"You heard me, woman. Get back here."

"I don't know who the hell you think you are talking to, Malik, but..."

"I know who I'm speaking to, and I'm telling you to get back over here. If you think I'm going to let you go into a situation half-cocked without a plan of action, you are out of your damn mind." I watch Vayda grit her teeth. She remains quiet as I continue. "Do you remember what we just talked about tonight?"

Vayda doesn't reply, but I know she remembers. "Prez is lettin' you sit in on church as a courtesy because Sydney is your niece, and he knows you are going to act whether or not you have the club's permission. The least you can do is work with us. It's not just you going in to get Sydney back; we all are. Without a plan, you risk not only Sydney's life, but yours and all my brothers. So, no matter how pissed you are at me right now, you need to sit down while we work together as a team to figure out how to bring your niece home. You can rip me a new asshole later."

Vayda takes a moment to consider my words. My calling her out like this in front of the guys will no doubt put me in the doghouse, but she knows I'm right, which is why she steps away from the door and makes her way back to her seat. When someone we love is in danger, we sometimes throw logic out the window. It's happened to us all. Hell, it's happened to me a time or two. Lucky for me I've had my brothers there to pull me back. Once Vayda calms down, she will see logic.

Thankfully, Riggs continues, and nobody acts as if I hadn't just royally pissed off my woman and landed myself in hot water. Although, I happen to catch a couple of *I'm glad I'm not you* glances from the guys. "Kiwi. Have you been able to tap into the feed over at the train yard?"

Kiwi grins. "Yep. Fuckers are smart. Whoever Cortez has on his tech team is good. Not as good as me though. They caught us by surprise, but now that I know what channel his guy is using to operate the override of the security system down at the yard, I can tap into his feed. His eyes are now mine." Kiwi taps the keys on his computer, and the TV splits into four different views of the train yard. "Bottom right corner you have the entrance of the yard. The Gate is closed. You'll notice here," he points, "there are two-armed men stationed there. Both wearing Los Demonios cuts."

Kiwi is right. The image is a bit grainy with it still being dark, but there is no mistaking the cuts the two men are wearing.

Kiwi continues. "Top right feed is of the control tower. It looks empty. Next to that, we have a view of the entire yard itself, and as you can see on the bottom right is what looks like an office. I'm guessing that it is in the main building."

"Wait for a second," I cut Kiwi off when I notice the door to the office swing open, and Cortez, along with two other men, walked into frame. One of those men has Sydney in his grasp. Vayda tenses next to me as she reaches out, clutching my arm. I place my hand over hers in a reassuring manner.

"Prez. How are we playin' this?" I ask.

"From the evidence, Kiwi has gathered, Cortez has two men at the gate, and two with him and Sydney. He didn't give us a location, so my guess is he's flyin' by the seat of his pants and doesn't have a well thought out plan. That and he might be callin' in backup."

"You think he's waiting on more men?"

Riggs nods. "I think that's what the bastard is doing. Only we aren't waitin'. We're going to ambush his ass."

"Fuck, yeah!" Nova pounds his fist on the table.

Riggs looks at each one of us men, including Vayda. "Suit up. We ride out in thirty."

Twenty minutes later, the guys and I are locked, loaded and

ready to hit the road. I look across the clubhouse to where Vayda is standing by the bar, strapping a holster to her thigh. She reaches into a duffle bag sitting on the bar, pulls out a pistol, shoves a clip in the end, checks the safety then straps her piece into the holster on her leg. Fuck me, I have never seen anything sexier than my woman preparing for battle.

Turning my attention away from Vayda, I look to Riggs. "Who's stayin' behind at the clubhouse to watch the women, Prez?" It hasn't escaped my attention Riggs has all us men suiting up. No way is he leaving the women and children unprotected. Just as the question leaves my mouth, Abraham LeBlanc, Riggs' grandfather strolls through the door of the clubhouse with his shotgun hoisted over his shoulder.

"I'm here for the party," the old man sing sings. I shake my head and eye my President.

"I called in reinforcements," Riggs announces with a grin.

"Hey, Pop!" the guys thunder in unison. Don't let Mr. LeBlanc's age fool you, the older man is retired military and an excellent shot. Also, Riggs has set up several tripwires along the perimeter of the clubhouse. Anyone who attempts to come onto the property will be picked up in pieces. There will be no chances taken when it comes to the safety of those we love, especially with Riggs' pregnant woman and Nova's daughter inside. As I walk out of the clubhouse behind Riggs and Nova, I steer Vayda over to my truck where she opens the door and climbs into the driver's seat, her demeanor full of grit and determination.

"Babe," I grip her chin, bringing her face toward me. "Stay close. Be safe and be smart."

"I will, Malik."

With my grip still on her chin, I bring her lips to mine. When we part, I step away. "Let's go get Sydney and bring her home." I close the truck door.

Mounting my bike, I fire it up. Riggs, who is beside me on his bike whistles, sticks his hand up in the air and gives us the signal to roll out. The rumble of our engines fills the night air as we ride out of the compound.

The streets of New Orleans are empty as we make the ten mile trek to the train yard. There is no hesitation, and there is no slowing down as we approach our destination. Kiwi, Fender, and Everest break off from us and turn right just as we hit Jasper Road. By turning right, they will breach the backside of the yard where the control tower is located while Riggs, Vayda, and myself will go in from the front. The plan Riggs laid out before leaving was to attack from both ends of the property. Kiwi checked the camera feed again before leaving the clubhouse, and there were still no signs of Cortez's backup. We have no way of knowing who or when his men will show, and no time to consider the what-ifs.

As soon as the gated entrance is in sight, Vayda, who is behind me and Riggs guns the engine, flies past us in the truck and aims for the closed gate. The two Los Demonios who are guarding the entrance appear and startle as they fire their weapons. Riggs and I reach into our cuts at the same time, drawing our weapons, returning fire. Both men go down just as Vayda drives the truck straight through the metal gate, breaking it open. Vayda drives several more yards before slamming on the brakes, bringing the truck to an abrupt stop in front of a large metal building, the one where we assume Sydney is being held. I pull my bike up next to the truck just as Vayda hops out. "Nice work, baby." Vayda and I take off toward the side of the building where we see a door with Riggs watching my six.

The three of us work together in unison just as we would in the field on a mission. Weapons drawn, Riggs and I stand at both sides of the door. Vayda stays to my right, watching our backs. I give Riggs the signal just before I breach the door by kicking it in. "Clear," I call out, and Vayda steps in behind me, followed by Riggs. The place is dark, and no sounds can be heard. Suddenly,

Kiwi's voice comes in over my earpiece. "I can see you, brother."

"Where are you, man?"

"I ducked down behind the tower so I could pull up my phone and access the camera feed. We took care of the two assholes out back. Nova and Fender are making their way toward you guys, and Everest is here covering my ass while I navigate you." I look to Riggs to see if he can hear Kiwi. He gives me a nod.

"Copy that, brother. Where is that motherfucker Cortez at?"

"Cortez is on the move. He and the other two guys have the kid and just left the office. You see the hallway about five yards to your left?"

"I see it."

"Down at the end of that hall is an exit. That is where they are headed. There is an SUV parked right outside the door. They're tryin' to make a run for it."

Riggs, Vayda, and I spring into action at the same time. The three of us maneuver through the darkened building and barrel down the hallway. We make it about twenty feet down the hall when I spot Cortez being ushered out the back by one of his bodyguards. With him a struggling Sydney. "Aunt Vayda!" she screams just before one of Cortez's men clamps his hand over her mouth. Being the tough kid Sydney is, she doesn't give up the fight. A second later, the man holding her bellows out a curse. "Ahh! You, stupid little shit!"

Sydney's action is just the distraction we needed. Because when the man loosens his hold on her, she breaks free and drops to the ground, right at the end of the hall. Cortez and the guy freeze momentarily. Not missing my chance, I take the shot I had been waiting for, and the guy who was struggling with Sydney slumps to the floor with a bullet in his head.

"Sydney!" Vayda calls out to her niece. "Run to me!"

At this moment all hell breaks loose, and the hallway erupts into gunfire from behind. Bullets begin to fly all around us, hitting the walls. Sydney's fearful screams fill the air as Vayda army crawls toward the frightened kid. Cortez takes advantage of the situation, scooping Sydney up around her waist, slipping out the door.

"No!" Vayda cries while ignoring the gunfire around her as she darts out the exit behind Cortez.

"Son of a bitch," I hiss.

"Move! Move! Move!" Riggs orders, shoving me into the empty room Cortez was held up moments ago.

"Fender and Nova are thirty seconds out," comes Kiwi's voice over mine and Riggs' earpiece.

"Copy," Riggs replies as I take out the empty clip from my pistol and load another.

"Cover me. I'm going after Vayda." I don't wait for Riggs' response before I dart back into the hall. My brother doesn't hesitate to unload another round while I make my way toward the exit. Shoving the steel door open, I step outside. That's when a metal pipe connects with my arm, knocking my weapon from my grasp. The blow does nothing to stop my forward momentum. It only pisses me off further. Twisting toward the asshole who hit me, I come face to face with none other than the President of Los Demonios, and I sneer. "Bad fuckin' mistake."

Gripping the bar, I pull, bringing the guy toward me. When his face is within reach, I bring my elbow down, splitting his cheek open, causing blood to run down his face. While he bellows in pain, I grab his left arm and twist. The movement causes him to drop to the ground. Using the metal pipe I disarmed from the motherfucker, I raise it above my head and bring it down across the back of his head. The blow I delivered was so powerful it caved in the side of his skull, leaving no question that the son of a bitch is dead.

Tossing the bloody pipe to the ground with a clatter, I retrieve my gun. Taking off on a jog, I turn the corner of the building to find Vayda struggling with Cortez, who refuses to let go of Sydney. As soon as Cortez is distracted by my presence, Vayda takes the opportunity to strike. Unsheathing one of the blades she keeps in her boots, Vayda sinks it into Cortez's side.

"Cunt!" he bellows, letting go of Sydney and backhanding Vayda across her face. That's when I take off across the lot toward my woman and the soon to be dead man. Hearing boots crunching on the gravel behind me, I glance over my shoulder to see my brothers approaching.

"Run! Run! Run!" I order Sydney as she darts past me and to my brothers, who I know will get her to safety.

Just as I'm about five yards away from Vayda, Cortez gains control of his senses, leans down and snatches Vayda off the ground, reaches behind his back for his gun and places it against my woman's head.

## 18

## TEQUILA

"You take one step closer and I'll put a bullet in her pretty little head," Cortez warns Malik as I stay focused on Sydney as she continues to run. Only when I know she's a safe distance from us do I show any concern for the current predicament I'm in, and the fact I have the bitter end of a gun barrel pressed to the back of my head. My scalp stings as Cortez's grip tightens on my hair. "You were all fools to think you would win against me. I never lose."

"Give it up, Cortez. Your first mistake was thinkin' you could waltz in here like you own the place, and fuck with my club and my family," Malik keeps his weapon trained on Cortez. "This is my city, motherfucker."

As the two of them exchange pleasantries, I slowly drop my arm to my side, hoping Cortez is too wrapped up in trying to prove he has the bigger balls right now to notice my movement. All I need to do is get to the three-inch serrated blade tucked in my other boot. Making eye contact with Malik, I then divert my eyes downward, trying to signal to him that I'm going to attempt to reach for something. If he knows me as well as I believe he does; he'll realize what I'm planning. Showing he understands, Malik remains focused on Cortez, never giving away the fact I'm silently communicating with him.

Malik takes a step to his right, causing Cortez to swing his weapon in his direction, momentarily giving me the small advantage I need to make my move. Bringing my foot up, I pull my second blade from the inside of my boot, twist my body into Cortez's, causing both of us to lose our balance. The gun in his hand discharges before he loses his grip, as we hit the ground hard with me landing on top of him. His eyes widen in disbelief as blood bubbles out of his mouth. The blade I sunk into the side of his neck throbs against the palm of my hand with every beat of his heart. I give the blade a twist, feeling it tear his flesh. Cortez gurgles as he chokes on his own blood. I find it fitting that the man who is known as The Butcher, the man known to cut up his victims, will die by the blade also. "Rot in hell, you sorry piece of shit." I twist the knife one final time before ripping it from his body. Blood quickly seeps from the gaping wound in his neck, pooling on the gravel beneath him.

Strong arms lift me from Cortez's almost lifeless body, and Malik pulls me into his chest. "Come on." He tries to walk me away, but I hesitate.

"He's not dead yet," I tell him, not wanting to leave until I know Cortez has taken his final breath.

Pointing his gun at the ground, Malik pulls the trigger, putting a bullet through the center of Cortez's forehead. "Satisfied?"

I look up at Malik's face; his lips turned up in a grin. "Now, you are just trying to show off."

Malik's hold on me tightens as he looks down on me. "Why don't you put that mouth of yours to better use besides tryin' to bust my balls."

"Why don't you kiss my—." Malik's mouth crashes down on mine before another word falls from my lips.

*This man.*

*My man.*

I deepen the kiss.

"Only you two would find the need to suck face in the middle of the battlefield," Riggs announces, letting us know of his presence. Pulling away from each other, Malik and I wait for him to make his way over to where we are standing. "Nice job," Riggs nods as he looks down. "One less piece of trash the world has to deal with."

"What do you want to be done with the body?" Malik asks Riggs.

"I'll make a few calls and make damn sure no one knows The Kings were ever here," Riggs mentions.

"Sydney?" my heart sinks with worry, and Riggs gives me his attention.

"She's safe. Nova used Wick's truck to get her the hell out of here. They should be at the clubhouse before we get there." Riggs peers down at Cortez once more. "And I suggest we do the same. The sun will be up in a couple of hours." Riggs turns and walks off.

Before Malik and I follow, I look up at him one more time. "I need a vacation."

Throwing his head back, Malik laughs. "I'll take you and Sydney wherever you want to go, baby." Tucking me into his side, we head in the direction Riggs is going.

"As long as we're with you, that's all that matters to me. I don't need anything more," I confess.

Fender and Kiwi are mounting thier bikes when we make it to the other side of the train yard. Placing his rifle into the carrying case strapped to his motorcycle, Riggs locks it shut. After getting on his bike, he pulls his phone from the inside of his cut. I don't make out everything he says other than giving the orders to clean the shit up, and make it look good, which I'm assuming has something to do with the dead bodies we are leaving behind.

Mounting his bike, Malik holds out his hand. "Ready?"

Placing my hand in his, I keep hold, swinging my leg over the back seat, then wrap both arms around his midsection. "Tighter, baby. Don't let go." Those five words hit me harder than anything he has ever said to me before. There is a deeper meaning to them.

Pressing my body closer to his, I grip him tighter than I ever have before, as his Harley comes to life. Bringing my mouth to his ear so he can hear my voice over the rumble of the engine, I let him know, "I'm never letting go."

Two months have passed since Sydney came into our live, and honestly, it feels like it has always been this way. It took a few weeks for things to settle down after Cortez and the Demonios bodies were found, and the media storm that followed his death afterward. The headlines read 'Notorious human and drug traffickers gunned down in the crescent city.' The official report stating a power struggle between Los Demonios and Cortez ended in bloodshed. I received an email from Scott the other day. He is still working on finding out who leaked valuable intel about my mission, which led to the capture of my team. All that matters to me is Cortez is dead. Also, Zara and her son are now free of that monster. She and her son are thriving. The Kings kept their word and protected them both. A few weeks ago the guys got Zara set up in her own little apartment here in New Orleans where she plans on staying.

Sydney is adjusting well. For a couple of weeks following her kidnapping, she had a hard time sleeping. Piper proved to be a massive help with getting her to overcome the fears by camping out at our place for a while.

Sydney finally got the call she'd been waiting for from her mom. After weeks of no contact with her, her mom informed us she could have visitors. As promised, Malik drove us to Nevada. The visit was only three hours long, but it was three hours Sydney needed. Georgia was looking like her old self again. She'd put on a few pounds, and you could see more than sadness in her eyes. I saw hope. Depression is a silent killer. I'm glad she's getting the help she needs. Not only for herself but her daughter as well. While they were visiting with one another, I sat back and watched, then the realization of Sydney not always being with Malik and I started to sink in. Her mom will get better, and Sydney will go back home. As happy as I will be for both of them when that happens it also saddens me.

I'm deep in thought when my dad pulls a chair up beside me and sits. "What's troubling you, Pumpkin?"

I continue to stare across his backyard, watching Sydney throw the ball to my dad's new companion, a German Shepherd puppy. I should have known something was up when I called him the day before we left for Nevada. I told him we would be staying for a night before heading home. While he was talking to his granddaughter over the phone, she told him she always wanted a dog. A German Shepard, to be exact. My guess is he got the dog for Sydney

"I was thinking about the other day. The visit with Sydney's mom went well. She looks better than she did before."

"That's good to hear. But?" he waits for me to give him more.

"I don't like the idea of Sydney leaving," I confess, then smile watching Sydney chase the dog around the yard, trying to get her flannel shirt out of his mouth.

"She'll still be a part of our lives, Pumpkin."

"I know, Daddy. It's just; I don't know. I like having her around. I like the routine we've fallen into."

"You mean you like having your own little family," my dad says.

I don't say anything. He's right. I have Sydney and Malik now, and even though I never thought something was missing in my life. They both make me extremely happy. I mean, the itch is still there to get back in the field again; to go out into the world doing what I do best. At the same time, I'm content with the simplicity of the way things have been since Malik and I came together. We've been not only taking care of my niece but each other.

"It's okay to want more than a career, Vayda. You can have it all." My dad pats the top of my hand. "Besides, I'm looking forward to having another grandchild one day," he adds, and I laugh.

"Don't get ahead of yourself. Malik and I haven't been together long enough to start thinking about having a baby. Besides, I'd like to have a ring on my finger before that happens. Isn't that what you always told me, Daddy. Marriage before babies?" I cut my eyes at him and smile.

He laughs. "That I did."

Malik steps out through the back door onto the deck. "Hey." He grabs my attention, and I lean my head back. Bending, Malik kisses me.

"Did you take care of the thing you said you had to do before we head home?" I ask him.

"Yep." His answer is short, and even though I want to ask what he was up to, I decided not to pry.

Sydney runs across the yard, the puppy hot on her heels, and jogs up the deck steps. "Grandpa, can I come to vista Misha anytime I want?"

"You sure can. Come to think of it," my dad shifts in his seat, "I meant to ask the two of you if you will dog sit for a couple of weeks?" His eyes dart from me, then back to Malik. "You see, the annual fishing trip the veterans take every year is in a few days."

All I can do is shake my head. He's a sneaky one, my dad. Proving my point that the very reason he got the dog was for Sydney. Now he's trying to find a way to make Misha hers, permanently. Sydney loses it. Most of the time, she's a chill laid back kid, but the mention of Misha possibly going home with us brings out girl squeals of excitement.

"Oh my god! Aunt Vayda, please?" Her face beams, and I don't have it in me to say no.

"Malik, what do you say?" I stand from my chair.

"I'm cool with it." He says, making one eleven-year-old girl very happy. She rushes to hug my dad's neck.

"I promise to take care of her while you're gone, Grandpa." My dad hugs her in return.

"I'm sure you will. Her leash is on the counter in the kitchen, and her bowl and food are sitting on top of the washer in the laundry room," he tells her, and Sydney is quick to run inside to gather everything.

My dad stands, and I embrace him. "I wish we could stay longer," I tell him. "Call me when you get back from your trip."

"I will, Pumpkin," he kisses my cheek, then faces Malik. "Son," he extends his hand. "Take care of my girls. Make sure to get them home safely."

"Always, Sir."

Loaded in the truck, Sydney in the back with the dog on her lap, we wave at my dad who's standing on the front porch as the truck backs out of the driveway. Before leaving town, Malik takes a detour. I look at him, confused. "Where are we going?"

"I need to make one more stop before we leave." Once he turns on Barnett Road, I realize where we are heading.

"Why are we at a cemetery?" Sydney asks from the backseat.

Twisting in my seat, I look at her curious face. "This is where your dad is buried, Sweetie." She peers out the window, becoming quiet.

The truck comes to a stop along the roadside. Climbing out of the truck, the three of us, plus the dog, make our way to my brother's headstone that sits beneath a large oak tree. It's been a while since I've come out here, but the fresh flowers and small unweathered American flag placed beside his headstone let me know it hasn't been long since my dad has visited him. I look over at Sydney and tears pool in her eyes.

"Do you think he would have liked me?" she questions.

Grabbing her free hand, I give it a gentle squeeze. "No doubt in my mind, your dad loves you. He may not be here physically, honey, but he is with you." Reaching out, I place her hand over her heart. "In here."

Sydney sniffles. "I asked my mom if she would take me to where my dad was buried. It made her really sad, and she started crying. I never asked her again."

"Depression is an awful illness, Sydney, so is addiction. If she weren't so sick, she would have brought you here."

"I know." Her face lifts. "But I'm glad I'm here now," she says before asking, "can I go sit in the truck for a few minutes?"

"Sure," I tell her, knowing she needs a little time to herself and watch her and Misha walk back to the truck. "I'll let you have your privacy," I tell Malik then start to walk away. He grabs me by the hand.

"Stay," he says. Turning around, I stand by his side as he begins. "I don't know where to start." Malik rubs the back of his neck. "I'm sorry, Damien. I'm sorry I haven't been back here since the day we lowered you into the ground."

It wasn't until now with his apology that I realized Malik stayed away for so long. I squeeze his hand, and he continues. "You were my best friend—my brother, and I let you down. The guilt of you dying eats me up inside. It should have been me that day. It's hard for me to feel any different, but I'm finally starting to work on it. I have your sister to thank for that." Tilting his head back, Malik closes his eyes. "You have a daughter. Can you fuckin' believe that?" Malik laughs through his emotions. "Damien, she is so much like you and Vayda. Strong, resilient, headstrong, loyal." He pauses for a moment, then glances at me. "I love her, Damien. I do." It's the first time I've heard him say those words, and my heart skips a beat. Malik looks back down, talking to the headstone. "You asked me years ago to watch after her if something ever happened to you. I kept my promise. Now, I'm here to make another promise I intend to keep. I promise to watch after her and love her for the rest of my life." Turning his body to face me, Malik drops to one knee, and I forget how to breathe.

Malik is about to propose to me, right in the middle of the cemetery.

"Oh my God. Are you for real?" Sydney screams, grabbing my attention. Jumping out of the truck, with the dog in her arms, she jogs toward us.

Malik gently grabs my chin, bringing my attention back to him. "I love you, Vayda Wilder." Reaching into his cut, he pulls out a ring box, and Sydney squeals again. I want to do the same, but I hold it inside. "I love everything about you."

"Everything?" I raise my brow.

Malik stands. "Yes. Everything."

"You do realize what you're getting yourself into, right? I'm a lot to handle." I smirk, and without waiting, he slips the diamond ring on my finger. Lifting my hand, I stare at it. A round diamond, set on a delicate gold band. Elegant, yet understated. It is perfect.

"I know exactly what I am getting myself into," Malik states, slipping his arm around my waist, hovering his lips over mine. "Marry me, woman."

"Aunt Vayda, come on. Stop torturing him already," Sydney says dramatically, and Malik grins.

"Am I torturing you?" I smile back and throw my arms around his neck.

"I wouldn't have it any other way."

"Yes," I give him my answer.

"Finally. You two are exhausting." Sydney sits the dog on the ground.

Malik pulls me close and cups my cheek. "I love you." "I love you too." Then he kisses me.

# EPILOGUE

## WICK

I stare down at the envelope in my hands with an array of mixed feelings swarming in my gut. It's the same envelope Damien made me promise to give Vayda the night before he was killed. I remember that night like it was yesterday, and the look of peace that came over his face when I made my promise to see that his baby sister got it. Eleven years I have been keeping the last words Vayda will get from her brother safe. Today I will live out the last promise I made to my best friend.

A rap on the bedroom door draws my attention, and I look up to see Riggs standing in front of me. "Hey, brother. Your folks just pulled up with Mr. Wilder. It looks like everyone is here."

"Thanks, man. I'll be out shortly."

With a jerk of his chin, Riggs turns and stalks back down the hall. A few weeks ago, I proposed to Vayda. We had taken Sydney to visit her mom in Nevada, and, on the way back home, we stopped at Damien's grave. I'd been planning to ask Vayda to be my wife pretty much since the moment I made her mine.

After I asked her father's permission, I didn't have any grand surprise proposal in mind. Big parties and public displays are not Vayda's thing. They're not mine either. But then came that moment we were visiting Damien and it hit me. I knew that was the moment I needed to ask her to be mine forever. There was no grand gesture, no crowd sharing in our private moment. It was just me, Vayda, Damien and his daughter. The moment was perfect. With my best friend and his little girl as our witness, I dropped to one knee and asked the woman I am in love with to spend the rest of her life with me. Now here I am, moments away from marrying the woman who means everything to me.

Standing, I tuck the envelope into the pocket of my cut and go in search of my girl. Shuffling out of the room and down the hall, I come to the last bedroom at the back of Pop's house. The door is partially open, and the sight before me knocks the air from my lungs. Vayda is standing in front of the bedroom window, peering out into the backyard as our family gathers to share in our day. The warm summer breeze causes the sheer curtains to flutter around Vayda's body. The afternoon sun peeking through the window where a sun catcher hangs, casts a diamond-like glow on her skin. Vayda is a vision in delicate lace. She's wearing nothing but a white bra that cups her tits perfectly while allowing her hardened nipples to peek through the thin material. On her bottom half, a white thong that barely covers her pussy, and leaves her ass bare. She's pure temptation for my dick, which, at the moment, is straining against the zipper of my jeans.

"Are you going to stand there all day and admire my ass, or are you going to come in?" Vayda sasses.

I push through the door and kick it shut with my booted foot. "I'm going to admire it, alright. I'm going to redden it with my mark as I bury my cock in your tight pussy."

Vayda turns away from the window, grins, and seductively sashays her way toward me, the sway of her hips, causing something primal to bubble in my gut. The moment she is within arm's length of me, I reach out and thread my hand through her hair, bringing her mouth to mine. I take her lips in a brutal kiss. Her taste explodes on my tongue, and I growl. "Turn around and put your hands on the dresser."

Vayda doesn't hesitate to obey. She braces her palms against the edge of the dresser. Fisting the tiny scrap of material keeping me from what's mine, I tear the panties from her body. At the same time, I unbuckle my belt, pop the button on my jeans and release my cock. A hiss escapes her mouth when I rub the head of my dick through her wet slit, causing her to rock her hips back, seeking sweet relief. "Malik," she groans. "Fuck me already."

The words barely leave Vayda's mouth as I thrust forward with brutal force, burying my cock balls deep inside her pussy. "Fuuuck." My head lolls back, basking in the feel of what has to be the closest thing to heaven I'll ever experience. Not waiting for me to move, Vayda begins rocking her hips, fucking herself on my cock. I grin. "That's right, baby. Take what's yours. Fuck yourself on my cock." I bring my palm down on her ass, marking it.

"Malik, I'm close." Vayda's breaths come out in pants.

I place my hands on both sides of her hips and halt her movements as I pull out of her eager pussy. A whimper escapes her mouth at the loss of our connection. "Come here, baby. I want to look at you when you come." I grab Vayda's arm and twist her to face me. "Hop up." I lean down, gripping her ass in both hands. Vayda places her hands on my shoulders and wraps her legs around my waist as I take three strides until her back meets the wall, where I swiftly impale her wet as fuck pussy once more.

After several minutes of working her body in a steady rhythm, I start to feel the walls of her heat flutter around my length. Reaching between our bodies, I find her swollen clit and rub it with the pad of my thumb. "Come for me, baby."

Having no choice but to obey, Vayda's pussy clamps down

around my cock as she comes undone, her cries of pleasure no doubt heard by everyone beyond the walls of this bedroom. With Vayda's pussy still spasming around my cock, triggering my own release, I let out a primal growl as I spill every last drop of my cum inside her.

Not wanting to leave her body just yet, I bury my face in the crook of Vayda's neck. I inhale her sweet scent as I allow my heart rate to slow, and both our breaths begin to even out. "I fuckin' love you."

Vayda peppers kisses down my face. "I love you too."

A few minutes later, after getting herself cleaned up, Vayda walks out of the en-suite bathroom to find me sitting on the edge of the bed waiting for her. "You want to go clean up?"

"No. I'm perfectly content wearing the smell of your pussy all day." I smile.

Vayda shakes her head and rolls her eyes. "You're too much, Malik. But I wouldn't have you any other way."

"Damn straight, baby."

I sit for a minute and watch Vayda as she walks over to her suitcase and plucks a pair of panties from the bag and slips them on. I take that time to pull the envelope from my cut.

"What's that?" she cocks her head to the side.

I reach out, thrusting the letter toward her. "It's something for you."

Vayda takes the envelope. "From who? What is it?"

The question dies on her lips when she recognizes the penmanship on the front of the envelope. She covers her mouth with her hand and drops to the bed beside me. "Damien."

"He...uh...he wanted me to give this to you on your wedding day. He wrote it the day before he died."

"Do you know what it says? Have you..."

"No. It's addressed to you. My only job was to make sure you got it. Damien was adamant you get this letter today should something happen to him."

Vayda sits silently as she stares down at the white envelope in her hand. Then she smiles, tearing it open. I watch as several emotions play out on her face. Her brow scrunches, she bites her bottom lip to fend off a smile, then the tears start rolling down her face. Finally, the last emotion is of pure joy, and without warning, she bursts out laughing. I'm talking head tilting, full-on belly laugh. I look on in part amusement, part confusion as she regains her composure.

When Vayda is done reading the letter, she swipes the tears from her eyes while holding the piece of paper to her chest.

"Everything okay, baby?"

"Oh, yeah. Everything is perfect." Vayda thrusts the letter toward me. "Here. Read it."

I take it from her. "Are you sure?"

"Yes. Please, Malik. Read it."

Doing as requested, I read what Damien wanted to say to Vayda on her wedding day.

*Baby Sister,*

*If you're reading this, then fate had other plans for me, and I am not there to watch you walk down the aisle and marry your soulmate. As I sit here on my bunk writing this letter while listening to my best friend snore, I know that even if I'm not there, you'll be okay. You'll be okay because Malik will make me proud and live up to his promise to look out for you. Not only that, I know you will be okay because you are strong. You, baby sister, are the strongest person I know. Your strength and determination are what I admire about you the most. As you read this letter while getting ready to move on with the rest of your life, know you and Malik have my blessing. If my intuition is on point, it's my best friend who will be waiting for you at the end of the aisle today.*

*I wish the two of you all the happiness in the world. No two people are more deserving of each other than you and Malik. So, go out there and live your best life, baby sister. Live each day to its fullest for the both of us. Let Malik make you happy and give you everything your heart desires, just as I know he will. Because Malik is the best man I know. Tell Malik he wasn't fooling anyone while growing up. I always knew my best friend had a thing for you. I knew he had feelings for you for longer than he's probably willing to admit. I'd also bet anything he gave you a hard time and fought that shit too. I used to get a kick out of threatening to kick his ass when we were kids. He's such a chicken shit. Ha. Ha. Ha. My best friend is loyal to a fault, but I knew he wouldn't be able to stay away from you forever.*

*And Vayda. One more thing before I go. Tell dad I love him, and I hope I made him proud.*

*Love Always,*

*your big brother*

*PS*

*Tell Malik it's about time he pulled his head out of his ass.*

Now it's my turn to burst out laughing. "That asshole."

"Can we get married now?"

Folding the letter, I hand it back to Vayda and stand. "Fuck, yeah. I'll be waitin' for you at the end of the aisle." I kiss her lips.

When I step out of Pop's house and onto the porch after leaving my woman to finish getting ready, I feel lighter. Somehow knowing I have Damien's blessing has calmed the storm and guilt that hadn't entirely disappeared from my heart. Sometimes closure is the greatest gift a person can receive.

"Ready, Son?" Mr. Wilder asks as he comes to stand next to me on the porch.

"I've never been more ready for anything in my life."

He claps me on the back. "Well, then. Let's get the show on the road."

Nodding, I bound down the steps and head across the yard toward the pier at the edge of Pop's property. The second Riggs' grandfather heard Vayda, and I was getting married, he offered up his place. I was shocked when Vayda happily accepted the invitation. I assumed she'd want to get married back home in Texas. She declined, stating that New Orleans was her new home. That here is where she wanted to build a life with me, Sydney, and the club. Vayda also didn't waste time planning the wedding. She, Luna, Josie, and Payton put everything together in less than two weeks.

Vayda said she had waited long enough to be mine and had made the joke that she wanted to tie the knot before I had a chance to change my mind. I ended up fucking those thoughts right out of her head when she made that remark. No way in hell was I changing my mind. Vayda was mine. Case closed. So, she and the girls went into full-on planning mode. To be honest, I didn't help much. I told Vayda to tell me when and where and I'd be there with bells on, and the rest was up to her.

When I showed up to Pop's this morning, the yard was transformed. There was a large table set up that could comfortably seat twenty people. It was draped in a white cloth. There was another large table filled with an abundance of food, and in the corner of the yard, my woman had the most important station set up—the bar. On top of all that, I caught sight of Josie and Payton stringing up lights or some shit on the bushes. I assume that was whatever girly shit the women wanted. That goes for all the flowery shit the pier and dock are draped in. All I care about is marrying my woman.

"Are we ready?" The pastor standing to my right asks.

I look over my shoulder to Riggs, who is standing beside me as my best man, then peer out at my brothers and my family gathered on the dock. I nod. The pastor gives the signal to Mr. Wilder, who is standing at the edge of the riverbed with Vayda, who has her left arm linked with her father and a bouquet of Lilies in her right hand.

Time stands still as I drink her in. My woman is wearing a

strapless white dress, flaring out at her hips, stopping just above her knees, showing off her long lean legs. My eyes continue to travel the length of her body, pausing as I take in her signature black combat boots. My eyes move back to her midnight curls that frame her gorgeous face. Vayda's whiskey color eyes connect with mine, and a smile tugs at my face. My woman is unapologetically herself. She is perfect in every sense of the word. The rest of my life begins the moment Vayda steps up onto the pier, and with a smile gracing her beautiful face, she makes her way toward our forever.